I WOULD
RATHER BE
A TURNIP

I WOULD RATHER BE A TURNIP

by

Vera and Bill CLEAVER

J. B. LIPPINCOTT COMPANY
Philadelphia   New York

I WOULD
RATHER BE
A TURNIP

CHAPTER ONE

NOW IN THIS summer of importance Annie Jelks was twelve years and one month old and her reputation, of which she had always been so careful, was being periled. Calvin, whom she remembered only as a little, squinch-faced, hairy baby, was coming to live with them. At this very minute Ruth was making ready the room he would occupy, digging out the old, caked dirt in the corners with a silver knife, sloshing soap and water around, squirting bug spray into the dresser drawers. All of the dark, make-do furniture in the room had been polished to a high, slick gloss. There were new muslin curtains with a red fringe and a new foam rubber mattress guaranteed for ten years.

Calvin was going to live with the Jelkses until he got to be a man. He was eight years old and in bygone days his relationship to Annie had been interesting; at school she had bragged to everybody about being an aunt. But now that she was over twelve and a little more knowledgeable it wasn't such a cheerful thing. For it had become known to her that Calvin was a disgrace to the Jelkses. He did not have a legal father; he had been born to Annie's sister, Norma, out of lawful wedlock. Mr. Jelks and Ruth, too, had tried to persuade Norma to marry the gangly, scared-eyed father of Calvin who had pleaded with Norma until he got laryngitis and couldn't talk any more but she had refused. It would be adding mistake to mistake, she said, and sat around growing Calvin until the day he was born and then she took him and went off to Hollywood, California, to be a secretary in a movie studio. Now Calvin was coming back to live with the Jelkses. He was due to arrive on the noon bus this very day.

Calvin knew how to travel by himself. According to Norma's letters Calvin knew how to do everything. He studied the encyclopedia and the dictionary and was going to be a doctor. He had a life-size, plastic man with numbered, removable parts which he could take apart and put back together again without even looking; he knew all the rightful places of the organs and could identify them just by feeling. Calvin was so smart he scared people.

It was ten A.M. on a hot July day. Hours ago Mr. Jelks had eaten his breakfast and gone off to his drugstore. Ruth had eaten with him as she sometimes did and hadn't bothered to clear the table afterward. The remains of their heavy, greasy meal sickened Annie just to look at it. Barefooted, dressed in a pair of old gym shorts and a sleeveless, unironed shirt, Annie stood in the doorway to the kitchen and smelled the smell of the cold, thick bacon and the coffee steaming on the back of the stove. Her father liked his coffee chicory-flavored so

8

that's the kind they always drank and Ruth made it strong enough to take the top of your head off. Ruth wasn't a good cook and she wasn't a good housekeeper. For as long as Annie could remember she had worked for the Jelkses. She came every morning at six and left every night right after supper. Now the sound of her song, raised in shrill, wandering lament, rasped Annie's nerves. She turned and went through the house and located Ruth.

She stood in the doorway to the room that would be Calvin's. "Do you have to beller like that? I'll bet they can hear you clean downtown."

"I'll bet they can, too," said Ruth. "I want them to. You eat breakfast yet?"

Annie locked her knees and fingered her stubbled hair. During one of her creative moods she had cut it to within an inch of her scalp, shaping it to a point in front of each ear and at the back and Suedella Jackson and Gwendolyn Ross had both admired her daring. But that had been a month ago. Now her hair lay, totally ambitionless, in ragged, dishwater-blonde rifts refusing to knuckle under to pins, comb, brush, or wave-set lotion. She grasped a front piece of it between her thumb and forefinger and pulled and rocked back and forth on her tough, bare feet. "I don't want any breakfast. You make my stomach so nervous with your bellering I couldn't eat even if I wanted to. If you have to sing why can't you sing quiet, pretty songs? Why do you always have to sing those loud, vulgar ones? This isn't Africa, you know."

9

"You don't say," said Ruth and went on with her mopping.

"Yesterday," said Annie, "I was over to Suedella Jackson's and I noticed *their* cook. She was so quiet you wouldn't even know she was alive."

"Maybe she isn't," suggested Ruth.

"She wears a white uniform and a little black apron."

"You don't say."

"Yes. I'm going to speak to my father about getting you a uniform. If he does, will you wear it?"

Ruth slopped more water from her bucket and with her mop stirred the puddle. "No, Miss Priss-Prass, I won't. I'm not about to wear a uniform. I like my own clothes. You better go eat. We won't have dinner 'fore one o'clock and you're going to get mighty hungry between now and then."

Annie left the doorway and went into the wet room. She pushed her feet over the wet floor and tested the mattress on the bed with her fist and walked around and around. "Calvin's coming," she said.

Ruth laughed and her long, lavender ears quivered. "Don't I know it?"

"It's a disgrace," said Annie. "I don't know what my father was thinking about. Calvin's a disgrace to the Jelks name."

The room went very queer and quiet. Ruth finished mopping the puddle. After a long moment she said, "You've been talkin' to that Suedella Jackson, haven't you?"

"Maybe I have and maybe I haven't," replied Annie.

"If I have been she didn't tell me anything I didn't already know. I know Calvin's a disgrace to us; I've known it for years and years. You think I don't remember the night he was born and somebody threw a rock through my father's store window with a note tied around it telling us not to show our faces in church any more?"

"That Suedella," said Ruth is a sad voice. "And her a judge's child. Somebody ought to wash her mouth out good with soap and then rinse it with vinegar. If she was mine that's what I'd do. What other lies did she tell you?"

Annie sat on the edge of the bed and dug her fists into the foam rubber mattress. "You think I'm a moron, don't you? You think I can't remember that far back. I can. I can remember every bit of it. Mrs. Jackson said—"

"Aha!" cried Ruth. "So she was in on this, too! I should have remembered Miss Suedella's memory isn't any older than yours. That Mrs. Jackson had better watch out what lies she tells about the Jelkses. She's got a few skeletons rattling around in her own closet that wouldn't stand any stirring up."

"What skeletons?" asked Annie.

"Never mind," answered Ruth. "I don't hold with gossip. The truth is more interesting any day. I'm just saying those Jacksons better watch out. If I told your daddy about this there's no telling what he might do. One thing's for certain sure; he wouldn't let you play with Suedella any more."

Annie drew her knees up to her chin and regarded her

feet. They were the largest feet of any girl in her class. Each year they grew another half inch or so and she couldn't persuade her father or the man in the shoe store that they didn't. "Mrs. Jackson's already told me I can't associate with Suedella any more," she said. "So my father would be a little bit behind the time if he said it, too. It's because of Calvin. Norma, too, of course."

Ruth said, "Oh."

"Is that all you're going to say? Just oh? If *my* favorite person told me what I just told you I think I might do something about it. I'd do something to revenge what had been said. I'd get a club and go after the blabbermouth. Oh, when I think of all Mrs. Jackson said to me yesterday I could just have a hissy! She made me suffer and it isn't fair. None of it's my fault. I can't help it if I'm related to Norma and Calvin. Can I?"

Again the room was extremely quiet. The mop in Ruth's hands went round and round and the puddle of water disappeared and there wasn't any sound to it at all.

Annie lowered her legs and let them dangle from the side of the bed. She rubbed the soles of her tough feet together and fingered her chopped hair. As in some far-removed time she heard the clock in the living room strike the half hour. "I just don't see why my father had to let Calvin come back here to live with us," she said. "It's going to ruin everything; it already has. Now I can't be friends with Suedella Jackson any more and tomorrow it'll be somebody else. Gwendolyn Ross probably. And after that it'll be somebody else and somebody else until all my friends have deserted me. It isn't fair. It isn't fair that I should have to have that little wart Calvin come here to live with us and ruin my reputation. Why does he have to anyway? Huh? Can you answer me that?"

Leaning on the handle of her mop Ruth seriously considered the question. After a moment of this she said, "It's because Calvin's not normal. He's too smart for his age and he's going too fast and he's got to be around some normal people like us to make him slow down. We're his only relations so naturally that's the first thing his mama thought of. He's just a little boy, Sugar. You got to remember that and treat him nice when he gets here. And don't pay any attention to them gossipmongering Jacksons. Their own skeletons won't stand any rattling so they just better stay home and guard their closet door unless they want me to deal with."

The children of the neighborhood had come from their houses with their dogs and bicycles. They were calling to each other and the dogs were yapping. The dogs and the children would race up and down the street in front of her house all day like maniacs, tormenting her. She wanted to be quiet. She wanted just to stay in her own room all day long with the blinds drawn and not eat anything or talk to anybody and not listen to any noise but this wasn't possible. All day long the kids and dogs in the street would scream and yap and Calvin was coming.

Because Ruth considered herself a member of the family she went with Annie and her father to the bus station. They sat on the hard benches and smelled the stale popcorn smell from the cold, silent machine in the corner and watched the travelers coming and going and each drank a Dr. Pepper and presently Calvin's bus arrived. He wasn't hairy any more. When Annie first looked at him coming down the steps, carefully holding his little satchel and blinking, she thought he didn't have any hair at all but then she saw that that was just a trick of the light. Calvin's head was covered with a fine, white down. He wore little rimless spectacles, white knee-length shorts, and a white pullover shirt. He was very dirty. He said he was hungry but not tired. He was very interested in the town. As they rode down King Street he stared out at it and asked questions. "What's the population of this place? How many hospitals do you have? Do you have a good library? Where's the library?"

Annie's laugh was loud and vulgar and her father glanced at her sharply. He drove around the corner and showed Calvin the library.

"I wonder how many volumes they have in there," said Calvin.

"Imagine," said Ruth, "a little boy like you asking a question like that. Now I think that's real remarkable. Calling books volumes and wondering how many there are."

"Probably not too many," said Calvin. "It's small."

"Yes," agreed Ruth. "It is that all right. Of course in a place like this maybe they don't need a big one. I just don't believe too many people in this town ever go there. I know I don't go as often as I should and neither does your grandfather because he's always so busy with his business and neither does Annie because she's always so taken up with her other doings." Regarding Calvin, her eyes were very sweet and gentle. She didn't make her nose flare the way she did sometimes when she looked at Annie. She began to tell Calvin how glad they were that he had come and what they were going to have for dinner and Calvin settled back and took a little piece of blue cloth from his pocket, removed his glasses, and thoughtfully polished them.

By this time they were out of the commercial section of the town and in the part where the homes were. There were sprinklers going on the lawns and children roller skating on the sidewalks and the air was thick and hot. They went down Cherokee Street and passed Judge Jackson's house. Suedella was sitting on the front step brushing her long, wavy hair. Even from the car Annie could see the gleam of her Vaselined eyelids. Annie shielded the left side of her face with her hand and stuck her tongue out as far as she could make it go and was pleased to note the expression of shock and disgust on Suedella's face.

"What was that all about?" inquired her father and Annie had to think fast. "Oh," she said, "Suedella and I belong to the same secret sorority and that was one of our signs. My, it's hot. I'm so hot I swear my bones are melting. Summers in this town are just pure, bloody murder. I do believe they get worse every year. I wish we didn't have to stay here. I wish we could go someplace where it snows. Alaska or Canada or someplace like that. Here I am over twelve years old and I've never

seen snow. I can't believe it when I think about it. Suedella Jackson's seen snow and so has Gwendolyn Ross.
All my friends have. I'm the only one that never has. It
makes my stomach squinch when I think about it."

"Then don't," said her father and turned the car into
their street. There were kids hanging from the fences
and perched in the trees. They hung upside down from
the branches of the trees with their mouths open and
their faces purple. They tightwalked the fences with
their eyes closed and their arms outstretched. There
were kids weaving around on high bicycles and kids
whizzing around on roller skates. A pack of joyful, yelp-
ing dogs raced from one group to another, vying for
attention. On a vine-shaded porch a pudgy saxophonist
in a baseball suit blew high, shivering notes. The street
was a sea of motion and the noise in it made the mind
whirl.

Annie put her head out the car window and shrieked,
"Shut up, you little brats! Stop that idiot screaming!
We're tired of listening to it! Go play someplace else!"

"How to win friends and influence people," said Mr.
Jelks and Ruth pounced on his remark: "Mr. Jelks, I'm
glad you heard her do that. I declare she's getting out of
hand. I think it's about time you and her had another
one of your talks; she's forgot about the last one. Did
you know she's taken to sleeping without any clothes
on? And yesterday she boiled her party shoes. That's
right; you heard me right. Yesterday, right after she
came home from playing with Suedella she boiled her

party shoes. The ones you paid twelve dollars for, Mr. Jelks. So I think things have gone far enough. I think you'd better have another talk with Miss Priss-Prass here and see what's eating her."

Annie's father wasn't being too attentive to what Ruth was saying. He was parking the car in their side driveway, maneuvering it until it was precisely beneath the kitchen window.

In the back of the car Calvin was standing. His little, brown face was sweat streaked; he was very excited. "Is this your house, Grandfather? I was born here, wasn't I? But I don't remember it. What kind of a tree is that? Don't you have a garage?"

"And besides that," said Ruth to nobody, "she's taken up smoking. She smokes cigarettes, if you please, and burns holes in her bed and someday she'll set the house on fire and burn it down and then where will we be? You have got to have another talk with her, Mr. Jelks, and find out what makes her so cussed all of a sudden; find out what's eatin' on her."

Annie's father and Calvin were out of the car. Mr. Jelks had Calvin's satchel and Calvin was skipping around investigating things. "Oh, what a pretty bush. I don't think we have any like that in California. And you have an outdoor fireplace. Is it to cook on? Good. Now just where are we, Grandfather? What street is this and how far is it back to town?"

Ruth was sitting very still in the back seat of the car and Annie was sitting very still in the front one. Now they were no longer friends. Ruth had tattled on her and this had never happened before. But what has happened once will happen again. History says so. Wars and people repeat themselves.

"I only did it for your own good," Ruth said. "You know you can't just go around taking your revenge out with smoking cigarettes and boiling your shoes and sleeping naked. You know you can't handle this thing all by yourself. You got to tell your daddy, Sugar, and let him ease things off for you."

The noise in the street filled her ears and the weather filled her eyes. "He likes Calvin," she said.

"Well, sure he does," agreed Ruth. " 'Twouldn't be natural if he didn't. But that doesn't mean that you and him have got to get a divorce."

Annie watched Calvin who had run over to squat beside the goldfish pool. His spectacles and his white head glinted in the sun. The bright fish, darting around in the water, seemed to fascinate him. "Look at him," said Annie. "Look at the way his stomach sticks out. He doesn't look healthy to me. For some reason I've got a feeling about him. He looks to me like he's got some kind of disease."

Ruth pulled on one of her gold-loop earrings. "Naw, he hasn't got no disease. All little boys' stomachs stick out that way."

"I think he's going to die," said Annie. "He's just got that look about him."

Ruth drew back. "He's not going to die. He's just a

little boy. If you're thinking along those lines you better stop it right now. I think you'd better talk your feelings over with your daddy, Sugar. Tell him about things so he can fix them for you."

"You shut up," said Annie. "Just shut up your mouth and keep it shut. If you don't I'll come to your house some night and cut your gizzard out."

She wanted only to sit in her room with the blinds drawn and hear nothing and do nothing and speak nothing but this was impossible. There was Ruth's hot, heavy dinner to be eaten and the table conversation swirling round and round and the noise in the street had moved up closer to their house. The noise came through the cracks of the walls even. Nobody seemed to notice it except her. They ate second helpings of everything and they didn't stop talking about California and Norma and the library and Mt. Shasta which Calvin had seen and the Pacific Ocean which Calvin had seen until the last cake crumb had been devoured and the last of the iced tea had been drunk. She didn't take part in any of the conversation. She sat with her feet curled around the rungs of her chair and stared at them and stuffed herself and she could feel her feet growing; they were never going to stop. She had a vision of her completed feet; it would happen when she was about twenty but by that time it would be too late. They would be as long as she herself was and she'd be a freak.

The food in her stomach was a great, hard, rock. She stood before the mirror in her room and bitterly re-

garded her image. She opened the top drawer to her
dresser and pawed through her collection of souvenirs.
There was a pointed lace collar which had belonged to
her mother and there was a pressed flower which had
come from her mother's grave a long, long time ago.
There was an oval tin box with a blue peacock painted
on its cover; once it had contained a silk handkerchief
with her name embroidered in the corner but now it was
empty. There was her baby spoon and her baby ring and
a picture taken when she was four years old. Even then
her feet had been too big. She had been ugly then as she
was ugly now. In disgust she closed the drawer and
leaned on the dresser staring at herself. She pulled her
lips back from her teeth and made her eyes wide. It was
just too bad she hadn't inherited some looks from somebody. Her father had looks and so did Norma. Why
couldn't she, Annie, have at least inherited a wave in her
hair? Or pretty ears? Her ears were too pointed and her
shaggy head made her think of dogs.

The dogs in the street were still yapping and even
though it was fiercely hot in the room she crossed to the
windows and closed them.

Without knocking Calvin came in. Coldly she eyed
him. "I didn't hear you knock."

He gazed at her through his shiny spectacles. "I didn't.
The door's open."

"Go back and knock, Calvin."

"On the open door?"

"You can close it if you want. I don't care."

Calvin went back out, softly closing the door behind him. In a minute he knocked and she said, "Come in," and he pushed the door open and tiptoed in. He stood in front of her, peering at her. "Are you sick?"

"No. Do I look like I am?"

"No."

"Then why'd you ask?"

"Because Ruth told me to. If you aren't sick why are you lying down?"

"Because I'm dying. I'm preparing myself for the undertaker. I thought it'd be easier for him when he got here if he found me lying down."

Like a priest Calvin laced his fingers and laid his hands flat on the round swell of his stomach. He had had a bath and now wore a pair of red shorts, a blue tee shirt, and a man's bush hat. One side of the brim of the hat had been turned up and on its crown there was fastened a round metal decoration. The hat kept slipping down over Calvin's forehead and he kept pushing it back. "You're funny," he said.

"Yeh."

"Aren't you going to ask me where this hat came from?"

"Calvin, I don't care where that hat came from. I don't care about anything. I'm dying. Can't you see that?"

"A friend of my mother's brought it to me. It's from Australia."

"Really?"

"Yes. I wanted a kangaroo but he couldn't bring it. He brought me this hat instead."

Annie sat up. "He?"

Calvin tiptoed to her dresser but couldn't see himself in the mirror because it was too high. He stood with his hands clasped over his stomach and the hat was down over his ears. "His name is Bryant Cape. He knows how to cook. Isn't that funny?"

Annie had risen. She stood beside her bed with her knees locked and pulled her hair. "This Bryant Cape. How old is he?"

Calvin thought. "I can't tell. I can't say. He's got a beard and he's from England. He can cook."

"Why, that's wonderful!" exclaimed Annie. "Imagine that! A man who can cook! I *like* men who can cook. I would never marry any other kind. And you say he's from England? Isn't that amazing? I'll bet if your mother marries him he'll take her to England sometime. He'll take you, too. You'll get to see the Queen. They have big libraries over there. You could find out anything you wanted to. Here they have just a little dinky one. You won't be able to find out anything while you're here. How soon is your mother going to marry Bryant? Oh, Calvin, just think! Now your last name is going to be Cape. You won't have to use ours any more. Isn't that something? Isn't that wonderful? Oh, I should write to Norma and tell her how happy I am for her. I'll do it right now. You wait right here and I'll go get some paper and a . . . what's the matter?"

"My mother," said Calvin, "isn't going to marry

Bryant. He's gone to England now. By himself. She didn't like him."

"Bryant isn't going to marry your mother? But you just got through saying he was! You just got through saying he came and cooked for you and her all the time! Didn't you just say that?"

"Spaghetti," said Calvin. "We didn't like it. It made me throw up. He didn't know the difference between a garlic bulb and a garlic clove. The bulb is the whole head and the clove is part of the head. He didn't know the difference. It made me sick."

The disappointment in her was so acute it squinched her stomach. Now she really hated Calvin and she let it show. "You spoiled it," she said. "Probably it was the only chance your mother'll ever have to get married and you spoiled it. You should be ashamed of yourself. I eat garlic all the time, bushels of it, and I don't throw up even when I want to. I think you're selfish, Calvin."

Hidden beneath the bush hat, Calvin's shaking head denied the accusation. "No, I'm not."

"I say you are. I say you're the selfishest person ever lived."

"There's no such word as selfishest," gently observed Calvin.

"Smart. You smart little pug-ugly. Little wart. Go away."

Calvin raised his forearm to his chin and smelled it. He nuzzled his inner elbow. "I got all my stuff unpacked. Come see it. Come see all my books and stuff."

"Books bore me, Calvin. Go away."

Calvin pushed his hat back. His bottle-green eyes were very grave. "Books bore you? I don't see how they could. I never heard anybody say that before."

"Go away. You're making my head ache. I don't want to talk to you. Go away."

She drew the window shades and lay on her bed and rubbed her tough, dirty feet back and forth across the clean spread. The dirt would make Ruth mad. There'd be a fight. She rubbed harder and breathed the hot, stale air and listened to the noise coming from the street. Presently she rose and went to the closet. She found her package of cigarettes and box of matches and returned to the bed. She applied herself to the business of smoking three cigarettes. She set her teeth and drew the hot smoke into her lungs and swallowed some of it and it made her cough and gagged her. She forced smoke streams from her nostrils and her head swam and her eyes watered and the food in her stomach lurched. She tottered to the mirror and with bitter satisfaction noted her boggling eyes and the queer green color of her face. The color was fickle; it was washed over with little waves of yellow. The pupils in her eyes were jet black. Something was going to happen. She turned from the dresser and started for the bed, staggering a little and gasping. Sickly through her mind there flittered a thought about the undertaker. His name was Pratney Apple and nobody liked him because he charged too much for his funerals. He smelled like fish and mouth wash and all he lived for was other people's dying. He'd charge her father too much for her funeral and there'd be an awful row because her father didn't like to be overcharged for anything; he was always writing letters to his congressman about taxes and fighting with the manager of the supermarket about spinach that had been watered down to make it heavier. Her father would have to pay though for her funeral and it would serve him right. Maybe he'd have to mortgage his store and fire Ruth. Ruth would starve slap-dab to death because nobody else in town would put up with her sloppiness and her bellering.

In this moment of illicit gladness Annie hobbled toward the bed thinking to stretch out on it and be dead when they found her. Everything was wavering and weaving. She couldn't see. The food in her stomach was sloshing. It was leaving her stomach and filling her throat. She reached the bed and weakly flopped on it. She opened her mouth and pulled air into her lungs. With her last strength she shrieked for Ruth. "Ruth! Ruth! You better come in here and see about me!"

CHAPTER TWO

SHE WAS ALLOWED to be an invalid for the rest of that day. She did not confess to the cigarettes and no one asked her about them. Ruth took the tray with the three butts in it away and wiped the spilled ashes. She opened the windows and a frail breeze blew in. She brought a radio and an electric fan from another room. She set a pitcher of chipped ice on the bedside stand and sprayed the air with Evening in Paris cologne.

From her bed Annie watched these occupations. "I suppose you phoned my father and told him I was sick."

Ruth flared her nostrils. "Sure."

"What'd he say?"

"He said he'd send something to settle your stomach. I told him you didn't have a temperature. You ought to sleep a little bit, Sugar."

Annie fished an ice chip from the pitcher and slid it into her mouth. Her feet, beneath the cool, smooth sheet, felt gritty. She wished they were clean but felt too weak to get up and wash them. "If I go to sleep I won't be able to take the medicine when it comes."

"It came a half hour ago," said Ruth. "I drank some of it. It's not nearly so bad as what your daddy made you take that time you tried to make us believe you were having a heart attack because we wouldn't let you go to the picture show with Willis Weeks."

Annie crunched her ice chip. With her tongue she pushed the shattered pieces of it back and forth against the roof of her mouth. "I don't remember that. You must be making that up. I wouldn't go to a dog fight with Willis Weeks. I don't know why you're bringing that up now. It was a long, long time ago. I can just barely remember it. Willis Weeks makes me sick to my stomach. All I can say about him is that he and Suedella Jackson deserve each other. I don't know why you brought him up now."

Ruth sprayed the back of her neck and the backs of her knees with the cologne. "I was just reminiscing, that's all. Remembering the other times you've been sick. We've been through a lot together, you and me. Remember the time your daddy went to Cincinnati to a convention and you got leukemia?"

"Aw now, that was just a story I made up and you know it," flared Annie. "I confessed it to you afterward."

Ruth was laughing. "I thought you were a goner that time for sure. You wasted away to skin and bones and you got so white I thought I was living with a ghost but you weren't any coward about it. I remember you only let me call your daddy that one time and then you stuck it out by yourself. You were the bravest little urchin I ever saw and I was proud of you. You remember how I slept with you every night?"

The ice in Annie's mouth had melted. Her tongue and gums were pleasantly cold. In the room on the other side of the bathroom she could hear Calvin moving around but he was being quiet. The street noises were far away and the electric fan on the dresser was whirring, making her drowsy. Her stomach and head felt queerly light and she wanted Ruth to lie down with her, like old times, but she didn't want to ask for this favor. "No, I don't remember. Maybe I should take a dose of the medicine if it doesn't taste too awful."

Ruth approached the bed and laid her hand on Annie's forehead. "You aren't sick, Sugar."

"Yes, I am."

"Want me to lie down with you a minute?"

"I don't care. You can if you want."

Still holding the atomizer and smelling strongly of Evening in Paris, Ruth sat down on the bed and then lay down. Her soft eyes were sweet. Like old times she pulled Annie close to her and began to softly stroke the thatched head and began to softly croon a child's lullaby.

"Not that one," whispered Annie. "It makes my heart hurt. Sing one of the songs from your church. The one about the snake who grew tame and was glad to be caressed."

Ruth's spongy bosom rose and fell. "I don't think I remember that one."

"It was about sin and a snake. He crawled down the

mountain and bit a lot of people but then he heard some-body speak the name of Jesus and he listened and grew tame and was glad to be caressed."

"Like some people," murmured Ruth.

"Yes. Like some people. I feel like biting people some-times. The world scares me now that I'm twelve. I think of how I'm going to look when I'm twenty and it just scares me. And I think of what I'll be when I'm twenty and it's just nothing. I'll be nothing."

"You'll be something, Sugar. Everybody's something. Don't worry about it. Go to sleep."

"Sing me the song about the snake."

"I don't remember it, Precious. I'm sorry."

Annie drew closer to Ruth. She turned her head and dug her chin into the soft fat of Ruth's shoulder. It was blissfully like old times when she had been forced to take naps in the afternoons and Ruth always lay down with her until sleep came. She slid her hand up and down Ruth's arm and found the familiar mole in Ruth's inner elbow. "People who smoke must be crazy."

"Yes," agreed Ruth.

"I don't know why they do it. Cigarettes taste terri-ble. Suedella knows how to inhale. She thinks it makes her look glamorous. It doesn't though. When she blows smoke out of her nose she looks like a horse."

"That Suedella," said Ruth.

"She and Willis Weeks are in love. She says that's what makes him so pale all the time. I don't believe it though. I think he's got hookworm. I think that's the reason."

"Love ain't anything to mess around with when you're just twelve years old," advised Ruth.

"Love is disgusting," said Annie. "It's the one thing I never want to experience. Just to think of it squinches my stomach. Love. Look what it did to Norma. And now we've got Calvin. It isn't fair for us to have to keep him and have everybody in town know about him. He should be sent to an orphanage or some place like that."

Ruth pushed Annie away and sat up. In one swift stroke the closeness and affection between them fled. Ruth's eyes were snapping mad. "You got no right to say your little nephew should be sent to an orphanage. You got no right to set in judgment on anybody. Nobody has. What if it was you who was Calvin? Just answer me that, Miss Priss-Prass. And he said *you* should be sent to an orphanage? Oh, you'd change your tune then! You'd scream your lungs out! They'd hear you all the way to Atlanta you'd throw such a fit! Because that's the kind of person you are. You're a fit thrower and all my years of trying to teach you to be good and kind have been for nothing. I see it now! I see they've all been wasted! Because you ain't ever going to be anything more than you are right now and that's a mean, cussed, selfish human. You aren't fit for decent people to associate with. Don't talk to me any more. Don't even look at me any more. I'm through with you."

Annie put her knees together and drew them up tight to her chin. Now she was glad the soles of her feet were dirty. She lowered her legs and rubbed the soles of her feet hard across the surface of the clean sheet. Ruth watched her. Now they were enemies again. After a minute Annie said, "Well, piffle." And that was all. She couldn't think of anything else fitting to say to Ruth. The situation called for a much stronger remark but she couldn't think of it and after a few more glares Ruth banged out.

Annie sat on the edge of her bed and dangled her feet and pulled at her hair and the child and dog noises in the street came back, louder than before. I will go crazy, she thought, and then I won't mind anything, not even Calvin.

She put her hands between her knees and closed her eyes and felt the noise running along the nerves of her scalp. It shouldn't bother me so much, she thought. Last summer I was out there hanging from trees and tearing around like a maniac myself. There is something wrong. This summer I am not like other people. It's because I am twelve now and know more and I am going crazy.

She listened for Ruth's voice and for sounds of life from Calvin's room. She rose and went through the bathroom and stood in the door of Calvin's room. Two concrete blocks had been brought in and across these two long pine boards had been laid. On the boards Calvin had stacked his books in neat piles. His plastic anatomy man stood in a corner of the room dangling its big, bare-muscled hands and shining its big, blue eyeballs. Its painted hair might have belonged to a man or to a woman. It was a queer sight.

Calvin was sitting in the only chair in the room reading. She went in and stood in front of the plastic man.

"Ugly," she said. "I don't know how you can be interested in such a thing. You must not be normal."

Calvin laid his book aside. He removed his spectacles and polished them with the little blue cloth from his pocket. "He looks different when all of his parts are in. I just stood him up there like that for the time being. His missing parts are in that box over there."

Annie went toward the box and leaned over it. She opened the flaps of it and after a minute reached down and lifted a cold, dark red organ.

"That's his liver," said Calvin. "Your liver looks like that. Mine, too. Everybody's."

Annie walked toward the plastic man. The liver in her hands was light but it was big; it was too big for the shaped hole she tried to fit it in. It wouldn't fit. "That's where his heart goes," advised Calvin. "See the numbers printed on his insides? Well, the same numbers are on each organ, too. The names are printed on them, too."

Annie turned the liver over. "It says here this thing's a hepar. I think you aren't as smart as you want people to think, Calvin."

There came Calvin's soft, penitent explanation. "Hepar is Latin. In English it means liver."

Obscurely she felt hoodwinked. Latin stultified her. *Amo, amas, amat.* I love, you love, he loves. A weird and useless language which nobody in his right mind ever would even try to comprehend or remember. What for? Would you ever, in the name of common sense, walk up to someone and say, "I amo you,"? Heck no. They'd think you had gone bloogy. She left the plastic liver sticking lopsided in the plastic man and drifted toward Calvin's books. "I am bored," she said. "And I am sick to death of things. I need to go away someplace where nobody knows me and I don't know anybody. If only I could do that; if I only could think of a way. But there isn't one. I'm stuck. Stuck good. I don't know why I can't be like other people. Other people go places and do things. They get all dressed up and go to the movies and parties. They have fun. They call each other up on the phone."

"I don't like telephones," said Calvin. "Neither does my mother. One time, when we first got our telephone, they gave us about the same number as a movie star and the phone rang all the time. It was never for us. It was always for the movie star. We tied a pillow around it so we couldn't hear it when it rang."

Annie stared at Calvin. "What movie star?"

Calvin crossed his little brown feet and polished his glasses. "I don't know. A woman. We saw her on television. She had lots of diamonds on and was silly."

"Ha!" cried Annie. "You think diamonds are silly?"

The expression in Calvin's eyes contained a secret. "Maybe not. Maybe they're all right. But I like books better."

Annie strode up and down in front of Calvin's dresser, watching herself in the mirror. It was late afternoon and the softening light did kind things to her face and hair. It glinted the blonde in her hair and lent hollow, interesting planes to her face. She turned sideways and looked at herself. Her neck was too long. Why couldn't

33

she have a short neck like Gwendolyn Ross? And teeth that didn't stick out? "I wish I had a diamond as big as this house," she said. "If I did I'd sell it, all but a big hunk to hang around my neck and a few little pieces for rings. *Then* you'd see me shake the dust of this town. I'd buy a Cadillac and a couple of those little dogs like women have. I'd hire me a driver to drive me to Paris, France, and that's where I'd live."

Calvin's gaze was dark. He was drumming the arms of his chair with his fingertips. *Rat-a-tat, tat. Rat-a-tat, tat.*

"I'd hire me some maids but they'd all be deaf and dumb. I'd live in a castle with a wall and one of those canals around it like queens used to have—"

"A moat," said Calvin.

"What?"

"You mean a moat."

"Yes, a moat. Calvin, you are driving me crazy with that noise. Stop it."

Calvin stilled his fingers. He pushed himself way back in his chair and then slid out to the edge of it again. "You couldn't drive to Paris, France."

"Why, I could so! Who's to stop me if I had the money and a car and a driver?"

"There is," said Calvin, "the Atlantic Ocean between the United States and France. So you couldn't drive there. You'd have to go by ship or a plane."

The room was odd and quiet. In the kitchen Ruth was making supper-preparation noises and the children in the street were calling to each other their temporary good-byes; they were answering the calls of their mothers to come get washed for supper. Calvin had his head in the crook of his arm and was looking at the plastic anatomy man. And the room was very odd and quiet.

Finally Annie said, "I didn't mean Paris, France. Did I say that? There's another place named Paris also and you can drive to it. It's by the ocean. That's where I meant I'd go if I had a diamond as big as this house. I'd get somebody to crack it up—"

"A lapidarist," said Calvin.

"Calvin, *will* you stop interrupting me?"

"It's a lapidarist," whispered Calvin with a guilt-ridden expression. "That's who would cut up your diamond. No, he wouldn't cut it. He would study it for a long time and then he'd take a special tool he works with and he'd just hit it once. That's how they divide big diamonds. I read about it."

"Well, piffle," said Annie. "I just can't think when I'm around you. You made me get Paris, France, mixed up with the other Paris and your talk about moats and that other thing is just too much. I wish it would cool off. I am just too hot to describe. I think I'll go down to my father's store for a while. Have me a nice, cold, ice-cream soda."

Calvin left his chair and went to his books. He knelt before them, contemplating.

She wanted to go to her father's store alone and mess around behind the soda fountain. She wanted to sit alone at one of the little marble-topped tables and sip her soda and read the latest movie magazines. And have strangers, passing in the street, look in at her and wonder if she wasn't somebody important.

She went to her room and put on the dress that made her look like a woman executive. It was black with white stripes and long sleeves. She put brilliantine on her hair and forced her feet into her black shoes. She went to the kitchen to tell Ruth she would be absent from the supper table. "My father and I will probably eat at The Dinner Bell. If not we'll just have a sandwich at the store."

Ruth looked at her. "Pardon my saying so, but that dress makes you look like you're a thousand years old. I told your daddy a hundred times you shouldn't be allowed to pick your own clothes and that dress proves it. You look like you just got out of prison."

Annie limped past Ruth and went around the eating table toward the back door. "I'll be back in an hour or so. You can tell Calvin. He's in his room reading."

Ruth jumped around the table, blocking her passage. "No you don't, Miss Priss-Prass. You're not going to leave that little boy here all by himself. You're going to take him with you. I've got an engagement which I intend to keep so you're going to take Calvin with you. I don't mind your coming in here announcing at the last minute that you're going to eat supper somewhere else but you're not going to leave that little boy here all by himself."

Annie stepped back out of the range of Ruth's vehement breath. Ruth had her back against the screen door and her glittering eyes and pushed-out mouth were silently rehearsing her part in the row that was brewing.

Annie locked her knees and squinted her eyes at Ruth and considered. If she took Calvin with her it wouldn't be so scary cutting through the vacant lots where old bums sometimes had been known to lurk. It wasn't likely that they would meet anybody she knew but if they did she could pretend that Calvin was a stranger to her, that he was someone she had just met. At the store he could stay back in the prescription department with her father. Anyway it was plain to see Ruth meant business. Ruth was capable of physical violence; the fuss she'd make if Calvin was left alone just wasn't worth it. "All right," she said. "I'll take him with me this time but just you don't go getting it into your head any idea about turning me into Calvin's watchdog. I've got my own life to live."

Ruth snorted and went after Calvin. He came from his room wearing his bush hat and lugging a book.

They left the house by the back door and went through two vacant lots.

Calvin had to trot to keep up with her. He wanted to know if, when they got to town, they could take just a minute and go to the library.

"Calvin," she said. "Is that all you ever think about? It's not normal for you to think about the library all the time and want to go there. You should be like other little boys and play with frogs and climb trees."

Calvin skipped around a low, spreading bush. "I play with frogs and snakes sometimes and I climb trees. I like

37

books better though. When we get to town couldn't we go to the library just for a minute? I have to find out something."

"Calvin, we are merely going to my father's store. Maybe we'll go to The Dinner Bell for supper but mainly we are merely going to my father's store. Stop pestering me about the library. Quit talking about books. Get your mind off books. It's not normal."

Under the bush hat Calvin's head shook his protest. "I will never get my mind off books. Never. I am going to read every one ever written."

"You'll go blind if you do."

"No, I won't. I've already read over a hundred. Someday I am going to write a book. Maybe I'll do it this summer. Grandfather has already said I could use his typewriter."

"We go this way," said Annie and they emerged from the last vacant lot and stepped out on the sidewalk. The town was just two blocks ahead. Under his hat Calvin was puffing but didn't complain. She made her steps long and he trotted along beside her, hugging his book. She darted a sidelong glance at him. "You don't have to keep up with me. I'm only walking this fast because it's the way I always walk. But you don't have to."

"If I don't keep up with you I'll get lost," panted Calvin. "What are all those buildings up there?"

"That's the town."

"It's little, isn't it?"

"Yes. Calvin, when we get to my father's store I want you to do me a favor."

"What favor?"

"I want you to take your book and go back to the prescription department and stay there. You can read and watch my father fill prescriptions. You won't be bored."

"No, I won't be bored," agreed Calvin and clutched his book tighter and they went past Professor Evans' music studio which was soundless and The Gray Moss Inn which had old people rocking on its porch; their thin, withered voices were like chickens cackling. The marquee lights of the Ritz Theater had been turned on; the girl in the ticket cage was painting her red mouth redder with a little brush.

The town had endured the heat of the day and now it was exhausted. The people wanted to be at home with their iced drinks and their air conditioners and their comfortable clothes and that's where they were.

Annie and Calvin went past the theater and entered Jelks' Drugstore. The air-conditioned coolness was in such sharp contrast to the outside heat that it made Calvin gasp. "Oh," he said, "it's cold." He went immediately to the back of the store where Mr. Jelks was working.

The long, cool store was empty of customers. Annie went first to the showcase where the perfumes were displayed. She selected a sample bottle of the most expensive kind and sprayed her hair and ears. Her father came from the prescription room to say that Jimmy Sass, the soda clerk, had the night off to attend a wedding. "Good," she said. "I'll clerk for you tonight."

"So we can't go out for supper," said her father. "You can make us a sandwich. I'll have a tuna fish salad and a vanilla milk shake with an egg in it."

"Yes, yes, I'll do it in just a minute. First I have to find a coat to put on. I don't want to get my dress dirty. Where does Jimmy keep them?"

"Jimmy doesn't wear a coat," was her father's dry answer. "He just wears an apron."

Annie had gone to a cabinet behind the cash register, was kneeling to rummage. "He should wear a coat. You should make him wear one. It isn't businesslike to wear just an apron. Oh, here are the coats, fresh from the laundry. Here's a whole stack of them."

In her green druggist's coat she looked professional. She walked the length of the store, examining the shelves of toilet aids and patent medicines, scowling at them, imagining what passers-by, peering in, would say of her. They would think she was a pharmacist and wonder at her youth. They would say, "She must be terribly smart. To get to be a druggist you have to know Latin first and you know what a hard language *that* is. They say she's a little on the peculiar side. There's a reason for it; years ago her family suffered a great tragedy—a scandal. There was a little boy born to her sister out of wedlock and the night it happened she was in this store filling prescriptions and somebody threw a brickbat through this plate-glass window with a note tied around it saying she wasn't welcome at church any more. So now the only person she associates with is her old, black servant.

She's very distinguished-looking, isn't she? They call her Doc Jelks."

There weren't any passers-by in the street. The movie-goers inside the Ritz Theater next door had paid their fare to see a double feature and there they would remain until the whole thing was over.

Annie went behind the soda fountain and made two tuna fish salad sandwiches and two vanilla milk shakes with raw eggs in them. She set everything on a tray and carried it back to the prescription department. Calvin was on a high stool in a corner reading his book; her father was taking drug inventory, recording names and figures in a ledger. "We could have come up front to eat," he commented. In his crisp green coat and creased, white trousers he looked more like a doctor than most doctors. The town people respected him; they called him Doc. People were always calling him up in the middle of the night to ask him about drugs and ailments. Every day he saved lives with his knowledge of drugs. He wasn't an ordinary man, her father. He could play the piano and do fifty push-ups without even breathing hard and could spot mistakes in doctors' prescriptions just at a glance. He had a beautiful tenor singing voice and one time saved a woman and her child from a burning building and got his picture in the paper afterward. The people in the town respected him but they didn't ask him to their houses to play cards on Saturday nights or invite him to be a Scoutmaster. Sometimes Annie felt a secret, angry pity for her father but she never shared this feeling with anyone. She had never spoken of it even to Ruth for two reasons; first, because it was impossible to understand and put into words and, second, because there was in the feeling some kind of trickery: Her father didn't need to be pitied. It would make him mad.

Her father was drinking his milk shake and eating his sandwich, being solemnly attentive to the food. He was making pencil doodles in the upper right-hand corner of his ledger and his mind was a thousand miles away. Calvin was chortling over something in his book. Annie went back to the soda fountain and made herself a chocolate ice-cream soda. She carried the tall, thick glass to one of the little tables in front of the store and sat down. She slurped her soda and lolled her feet and shrewdly considered the long, hot summer that lay ahead. Unless she could think of a way to overcome the stigma of Calvin the summer would be a mean one; she'd be left out of everything and the days would stretch from morning to night with nothing to relieve the futile hours except fights with Ruth and even these, of late, were losing their flavor. Lately Ruth's side of their fights were serious; she couldn't be coaxed to see the funny side of them afterward but sulked and growled and made up all kinds of new, impossible rules. So the summer would be tasteless and friendless. On Mondays there would be her piano lessons: The metronome clacking away on top of the piano and Professor Evans clacking his porcelain teeth and shivering his disapproval. In August she was going to be in a piano recital and play the ghastliest piece ever composed, a long, chromatic diatribe which nobody but a deaf mute could sit through without getting strained jaws. It would be held at the Women's Club House and she'd have to wear a dress of Ruth's choice (tan or light blue probably) and her father would be expecting her to outdo Shack Vareen who had long yellow curls and was a child prodigy. Calvin would be there, too, of course, for everybody to look at and whisper about. Unless she could think of a way to get rid of him.

She had drunk all of her soda and eaten all of the ice cream in it without tasting it. Feeling vaguely cheated she rose and went to the magazine rack near the door and selected two movie magazines. She riffled through these quickly, looking for pictures of her movie idols. They were both dark men with dimpled chins and deep, lonely eyes and were the only things she and Suedella Jackson and Gwendolyn Ross had never disagreed on. Neither of their pictures were in the magazines. She returned them to the rack and went back to the soda fountain. She squirted cherry syrup into a sundae glass and thoughtfully held the glass under the carbonated water tap until it ran over. The pink, fizzed water was pretty.

Back in the prescription department Doc Jelks and Calvin were very quiet.

At the street door there was a sudden commotion; there was Suedella Jackson and Gwendolyn Ross escorted by Willis Weeks and Lamar Dandridge. Suedella had on a purple dress and purple eye shadow and little purple shoes. She came tripping in ahead of the others and went directly to the cluster of tables and selected

43

one. Willis held her chair for her and she slid into it without any fuss. Gwendolyn and Lamar were laughing; they were all talking about the movie they had just seen.

Hating them, Annie stood in back of the soda fountain. She made another pink fizz in the sundae glass and after the bubbles had stopped working poured it out. From the prescription department her father called to her to wait on the customers and finally she came out from behind the fountain and went over to them. She stood at their table with her knees locked and her hands clenched inside the pockets of her druggist's jacket. Willis was paler than she had ever seen him. His white, fine skin was almost translucent; Annie could almost see the blood running in the veins beneath it. Suedella was beautiful; she had pearls twisted in her long, brown hair.

Suedella said, "Order for us, Willis." And Willis jutted his jaw and cracked his knuckles. "Yes," he croaked. "Oh, ah, four hot fudge sundaes with butter pecan ice cream."

"No butter pecan," lied Annie. "Just vanilla. And no hot fudge either."

The four conferred and while they were doing this Calvin came from the prescription room and went wandering up and down the aisles pausing every foot or so to read the labels on the patent-medicine bottles. He drifted toward the soda fountain and went behind it. His head was hidden under his bush hat and the soda fountain, tall as it was, hid him. His voice came as something not connected with anything real: "Annie, I want a drink of water, please."

"We'll all just have a dish of vanilla ice cream," said Willis.

Suedella was looking at Annie. Her lustrous eyes and her painted mouth were slyly without expression. "I didn't know you were working for your father this summer, Annie."

Annie fixed her eyes on the pearls in Suedella's hair. They were cheap—imitation and not very well strung. At one point along the strand there was an empty space half an inch long. They were beautiful. She said. "I'm not working for my father this summer. I'm just doing it tonight." She turned and started away from the table and felt all their eyes on her back. She felt them leave her back and go to Calvin and she heard their whispers.

In back of the fountain Calvin had dragged something to stand on up to the middle part of it where the water taps were and had climbed up to draw his own glass of water. He was drawing the water from the carbonated tap and it was spraying the front of him. He had taken his hat off and he looked like a little, wet professor. Inspiration seized her. She turned and went back to the table. She stood over the four who at one time had been her friends and it was a necessity with her that if they were not to be friends any more she should be the one to say it wasn't possible any longer. She looked into their courteous, shifty faces and she said, "I *could* work for my father this summer if I wanted to. He offered me

45

twenty-five dollars a week. But I'm busy with a more important project. I am writing a book."

The four at the table did not look at each other; they didn't smile or laugh. They just sat, patiently waiting for their ice cream.

"It's going to be a big, thick one," she said. "I'm typing it to make it easier to read. Probably I'm going to sell it to the movies when it's finished. I have a distant relative who works for a movie company out in Hollywood, California, and she said that's where they get their ideas for movies; from books. Mine is going to be about five hundred pages long."

At last one of the four at the table spoke. "I didn't," said Suedella, "know you knew how to type."

The braggart and liar in Annie spoke for her: "Sure I do. I just never mentioned it to you, that's all. I can type almost two hundred words a minute. I taught myself on my father's typewriter. I'm glad I do know how; if I didn't, writing my book would be an awful job."

Suedella and Gwendolyn and Willis and Lamar controlled their disbelief and their amusement. They put their hands in their laps and waited for her to bring them their ice cream.

She could feel her face redden and she felt for all of them, but for Suedella most of all, an intense hatred. She left their table and went to the soda fountain and set out four glass ice-cream dishes. She drew four glasses of water and set these on a carrying tray. Calvin had climbed down from getting his own drink of water and stood leaning against the refrigerator box where the ice cream was kept. He was somberly watching her. She took an ice-cream scoop from its well, flipped open the lid to the ice-cream compartment, dug the scoop into the hard, white cream.

Calvin had a folded, paper napkin in his hand; he was protecting something inside the folds of it. With bright interest he was watching her dig the ice cream from the carton. "Are those people your friends?" he whispered. "That girl with the pearls in her hair. Is she?"

"I hate her," answered Annie.

Behind his little rimless spectacles, Calvin's eyes were softly shining. Tenderly he extended the folded napkin and tenderly he opened the folds of it to show her the dead cockroach inside, darkest brown with long, thread-like antennae and gleaming, leathery integument. "I found him on the floor," he whispered. "Put him in that girl's glass. Way down at the bottom. Push the ice cream around him so she won't notice him until she's almost finished eating it."

Annie's eyes locked with Calvin's. After a second or two she took the napkin from his hand, shook the dead roach from it into one of the ice-cream dishes, scooped a round ball of cream and deposited this on top of the dead insect.

"He shows," whispered Calvin, peering. "I can see him from the outside. Cover him up good; tuck him in."

Annie tucked the cockroach into the ice cream, picked up the tray, and carried it over to the table where her four former friends waited. She served Sue-della first. She watched Suedella pick up the spoon. She

47

served the other three very quickly and then went back to the prescription department. She stood at her father's elbow, watching him write in the drug ledger. She waited for Suedella's scream of horror and outrage and it came.

CHAPTER THREE

THE WORLD BORED HER with its everyday certainties. The sun rose and Ruth came to work. Her father ate his breakfast and went to his drugstore. The yardman came and mowed the yard and cleaned the goldfish pond. Ruth served him big lunches. In the afternoons he dug around the flower beds and watered the grass and shrubs. One of his arms was shorter than the other and he looked very old and wise and calmly satisfied.

In his room Calvin played with his plastic anatomy man and burrowed his head in his books and had private conversations with Ruth. He was never bored.

There had been other times in her life when she had been uncomfortable — little, short periods when she had waited for people and things to settle down and be right with her. This time it was different. This time she wasn't going to get better. Now she was older and wiser and couldn't go out into the neighborhood and giddily hang from trees and walk fences making new friends while waiting for her old ones to come back to her. This time they weren't coming back. Now Suedella Jackson and Gwendolyn Ross walked past her house on their way from town, swinging their peppermint-striped shopping bags, tossing their fluffy heads, laughing, and never even glancing toward the Jelkses' house.

She wandered around through the rooms of the house and in and out of it, pulling at her hair and making plans that never materialized. At mealtimes she sat at the table with Ruth and Calvin, staring at her feet and stuffing herself with Ruth's listless food. Whenever the phone rang she'd run to answer it but it would never be for her.

"I thought you were going to write a book," said Ruth. "Didn't you tell that bunch you used to rare around with you was going to? Didn't you tell them you could type two hundred words a minute and were going to write a book?"

On this day Annie did not see anything sweet or motherly in Ruth. Ruth was a busybody spyer, a sneak with incredible, X-ray ears. Her ears could hear things that were being said ten miles distant and her eyes could see around corners.

Annie averted her gaze from the ugliness of Ruth. "Who told you I said that?"

"Oh, people tell me things," replied Ruth. "I hear things even when I'm not listening for them. If you're going to make that lie come true you'd better get busy. Even Norma can't type two hundred words a minute."

"Because she's stupid," said Annie. "She's made a mess out of her life and now she expects other people to bear the blame for it. Oh, I am sick to death of everything."

Ruth's laugh was extravagant; it showed all of her

teeth which were as white as candles. "If you going to make that lie of yours even one-third true you better get busy. There should be a typing book around here somewhere; it belonged to Norma. Want me to find it?"

"I'm not crippled," said Annie and went to Norma's old room which still smelled like Norma — like fresh lemons and sensible hand lotion. After all the years that had passed it still smelled like that. The room was like Norma; it was clean and strangely cool. The bed that Calvin had been born in stood against the wall. Annie did not look at the bed. She went through the drawers and the closet methodically, looking for the typing book but did not find it.

"Well," said Ruth, "the words that was in it wasn't anything unusual. I see the same ones in the newspaper every day."

"You have to know how to hold your fingers," whispered Calvin. "Bryant Cape showed me. And then I practiced every day until I could do it. See? You hold your fingers like this. You hold this finger on j and this finger on f and then you go back and forth and up and down. It's easy after a while. See? Like this."

Annie sat before the typewriter in the cloying warmth of her father's room which was half office and slowly, painfully copied lines from the town's weekly newspaper: MIsx Arlene Jane Callicott became the bride of Coochie George jr in a 5 o%ck%tg ceremony 78456& at thr FIrST baptist ey7dg. Mrs. 75d Keith Clay visited LAst week with her sister, Mrs. &83jQ9o2.

Calvin was leaning against the typing table watching her. He was drumming against the surface of the table with his fingers. *Rat-a-tat tat. Rat-a-tat tat.* He had his teeth clenched and his eyes closed. He had been standing there for a long time without saying a word.

There was sweat in her hair and in her eyes. She memorized another line from the newspaper and applied herself to the business of typing it. u8s ETHel stroup was a week_end guSt in the homeof her parents, *f* Dr. and iot STroup. She stared at the typed words. "Well, it's not perfect but it's not so bad either. You can't expect me to be perfect in just half an hour."

"We've been here two," whispered Calvin. "Let me type now."

"I don't," said Annie, "know why they print such stuff in the newspaper. Who cares who got married and who visited who? It's not even interesting."

"Let me type now," whispered Calvin. "It's my turn now."

"Newspapers are supposed to tell about important stuff. This makes me sick to my stomach. The people in this town are nothing but a bunch of fool baboons."

Calvin opened his eyes and looked at her; the expression in them was gravely anxious. "Baboons are smart. They're almost like humans."

"They're like stupid mules. *Hee-haw. Hee-haw.* You hear one doing it and they all do it. *Hee-haw. Hee-haw.*"

"Type some more," said Calvin.

"Go away. You're bothering me."

"No, I'm not. I'm standing here watching. When are you going to start your book?"

"Right now."

"What's it going to be about?"

"I don't know yet. I haven't decided. Go away. You're bothering me."

Calvin sat down in Annie's baby rocker which had been brought in to the room by Ruth. He folded his hands across his stomach and rocked and waited and the long, mauve shadows of the waning afternoon gathered in the corners of the room.

Annie gnawed her lips and fingered the stubbled growths of her hair and considered this book of hers she was about to write. It should be simple and lovely and get to the point at once. It should be about snow and leaves and birds. The birds could look like people and talk like them. Buzzards were strong, mean-looking birds. Maybe her story shouldn't be simple and lovely. Maybe it should be about two buzzards who looked like people. She would have to make them do something interesting, but what was interesting?

Calvin had left the room to go after a book but now he was back. He was rocking and reading and making soft, little nickering sounds with his mouth.

Ruth came and stuck her head in the door and didn't say anything. She went away.

The blank sheet of yellow paper in the typewriter stared back at Annie. She blinked at it and the uneasy knowledge of her possibilities seemed somehow menacing.

Annie stared at the sheet of blank paper in the typewriter. This writing of a book wasn't going to be such an easy business.

She let her eyes wander to Calvin's bent head, shining like tinsel in the under-dusk of the room and something warm and rich and buoyant swept across the surface of her mind. A pale, floating phantom appeared and gathered itself into a definite shape. Something spoke to her. She lifted her hands to the typewriter keys and began page one of her book. The words poured out of her mind and her fingers transferred them on to the paper. It was a miracle.

She created Cordelia, a young girl with beautiful yellow hair and eyes the color of wine. In her village she stood out like a queen with manners of lovely grace. She *was* a queen, exiled from her tiny, native European country by raiders who came riding a hundred strong one morning up over the sweet hills and down through the meadows and when they reached her father's castle, there they did some things that not even they could talk about afterwards.

Cordelia alone made her escape to the highlands where a kindly farm couple gave her shelter.

There was a river in this story which ran like a shiny snake through the valley beneath the house where Cordelia had been given refuge. The land was sweet with some green ponds and low, crumbling walls. Wild roses bloomed everywhere. There were two church spires, proud and simple, and there was the sound of the Angelus bell, calling the people to prayer. And there was Cordelia, lonely and grieved, standing on a hilltop at twilight, her lovely face yearning, ever turned to the west which was the direction she had come from.

Annie progressed in the beginning of this writing very fast. It was unreal; it almost wrote itself. As fast as she could type, Cordelia leaped out of her brain and came alive on the yellow paper. Within the space of an hour she had two pages.

But then something happened. A shade came down over the pictures in her mind and the words choked and sputtered and stopped coming.

"It's because you're hungry," said Ruth. "Come and eat."

She sat in the kitchen with Calvin and Ruth and solemnly ate two baked sweet potatoes. She returned to her typewriter. She pulled her hair and chewed her lips and scoured her mind for excellent words and beautiful thoughts and after a while a few came but they didn't set the story in motion again. Cordelia was rooted to the hilltop and now her plight seemed artificial and unimportant. Dumb even. Who the heck would want to read about such a girl? Where was her gumption anyway? Instead of standing around on hilltops squalling and grieving over things that couldn't be helped why didn't she go into the town, even if she had to walk, and get herself a job? Why hadn't she saved some of her money while she was queen? Oh-oh, how *could* she have been queen if her father had been king? She wasn't her father's wife;

she was his daughter. Rats and piffle. Now it was all mixed up.

From her yellow pages Cordelia looked up at Annie, an inscrutable smile on her lovely lips.

While Annie was trying to decide whether to make an attempt to save Cordelia or just let her stand on the hilltop forever, Calvin, dripping orange Popsicle, drifted in. He sat in the little rocker and rocked back and forth and gazed at her. "Grandfather won't be home until eleven o'clock."

"Really?"

"He phoned. I talked to him. You learned to type fast."

"Yeh."

"Are you writing your book now?"

"Yeh."

"What's it about?"

"A queen."

"What queen?"

"Just a queen."

"What country is she queen of?"

"Calvin, I don't know. I haven't got to that part yet."

Calvin licked his orange lips with his orange tongue. "I don't like to read stories about queens. What's her name?"

"Cordelia."

"A queen named Cordelia," said Calvin with specks of real distaste in his green eyes. "It makes me think of something I don't like. Jam with seeds in it, that's what it makes me think of. Jam with seeds in it. I don't like jam with seeds in it. I like plain jam. Why don't you make her name Mary or Dorothy or Norma?"

"Because her name's Cordelia, Calvin."

"Queens are lazy."

"This queen's not."

"All they do is lay around all day long and have people wait on them. They're lazy."

"Calvin, you have the queerest ideas. You don't know anything about queens. You're too little to know anything. Queens do *not* lay around all day long having people wait on them. My queen isn't doing that. Right now she's having to live with a farm couple. In a minute I'm going to put her to work. She'll have to work from the time the sun comes up till it goes down. It'll be hard; she's going to make goat cheese with straws in it."

"What're the straws for?"

"To let people who come to buy the cheese know it's been made by farm people. Everybody likes stuff that comes from a farm. That's why I'm going to put that in there. Somewhere I read about people in Europe putting straws in cheese."

There was strong rejection in Calvin's little brown face. "I don't like your story. I don't like to read about queens. Ruth's gone home and there are some girls walking up and down in front of this house. One of them called me a name."

Annie looked at Calvin hard. "What name?"

Calvin shrugged. "I don't know. It was something I never heard before. Can I type now?"

Annie relinquished the typewriter to Calvin. She went

57

through the quiet, darkened house and out on the porch. The street lights had come on; the air was thick and sweet with the smell of night-blooming jasmine. Suedella Jackson and Gwendolyn Ross were walking up and down in front of the Jelkses' house. With their arms linked and their heads bent they walked slowly. Suedella's hand lightly trailed the picket fence and with each step her pale skirt billowed prettily.

The scent from the white, flowering jasmine bushes was overpowering. The yellow glow from the street lights hanging from their lampposts colored the sidewalk beyond the fence. The light seemed to follow the two girls walking slowly along the sidewalk outside the Jelkses' fence.

Queerly, Annie felt a little tug of something like fear. It was so queer and quiet, their walking up and down out there like that. She went to the edge of the porch and called to them. "Hey."

Abreast of the gate they turned and stopped. The light from the street lamp fell across their faces. "Hey, Annie."

They were going to be friendly; they had come back to her. She felt things settle and right themselves. She ran down the steps and to the gate. "I've learned to type and I'm writing my book! Oh, wait'll you see it! It's about a queen and her name's Cordelia. What are you doing? Are you going someplace? Want to come in and see me for a while? We could watch television."

They had their hands on the pointed pickets of the

gate and they were looking at her in a funny way. Their faces were shiny and their shiny lips were pink and soft and their shiny eyes were pure. "No," they said. "We can't come in to see you. We can't go inside your house; we promised our mothers."

She said, "Oh," and took a step backward.

"Thing's have changed," said Suedella. "I mean, even before you put the roach in my ice cream they had."

"That wasn't anything," said Gwendolyn. "That was a mere nothing."

"You know why," said Suedella, as if dispensing a lesson. "You remember we talked about it last time you were over to my house."

"Yes," agreed Annie. "But it isn't my fault. None of it's my fault. Look here—"

"You're Norma's sister," continued Suedella. "You might be like her now that you're old enough. That's all we're saying."

"I'm not like her! I couldn't be! Now you look here!"

"We only," said Gwendolyn, "were walking by. We have to go now." They let their hands drop away from the top of the gate. Their smiles were pleasant and blank as air. Taking light little steps they moved away from her, went across the section of grass between the sidewalk and the curb. At the curb they stopped and looked in both directions and then stepped down.

She opened the gate and stood between its two posts and roared at them. "Baboons! Fool baboons! Mules! *Hee-haw! Hee-haw! Hee-haw!* That's all you know how to do! You called Calvin a name and I'm going to have you arrested! As soon as I tell my father he'll have you arrested!"

They turned and came back. They stood on the section of grass between the sidewalk and the curb and they spoke in a sad way. "We only," they said, "called him what he is. How can we get arrested for that?"

"Baboons! Mules! *Hee-haw! Hee-haw!*"

Before they walked away into the calm, scented night Suedella spoke the name that belonged to Calvin. "It's what he is," she said. "So how can you get us arrested for saying it?"

"*Hee-haw! Hee-haw!* Baboons! Mules!"

They were walking away from her. Their little heels tapped *click, click* on the pavement and the wind lifted their hair and then the night swallowed them.

It was ten o'clock and Calvin had put himself to bed. Dressed in red pajama bottoms he lay motionless between the sheets, fists curled, one arm crooked around a book. His bare chest was brown and sweaty; he smiled sweetly in his sleep.

She stood over him and in the silence of the house and in its darkness she heard her heart beat. She stood motionless, watching Calvin sleep and watching the curtains at the windows blow inward. There was trapped air inside her lungs and she expelled it slowly and evenly. There were such thoughts in her head, such big and evil ones that not even to herself did she dare express them.

In his sleep Calvin rolled over.

She went back to her own room. She turned on the overhead light and the light on the stand beside her bed. She switched on the radio as loud as it would go and walked around and around. Her knees hurt her and her head ached. She wanted sleep but she was afraid to lie down and close her eyes.

CHAPTER FOUR

FOR DAYS AFTER that she found it hard to look at Calvin directly and to look at herself in the mirror. She hated what she saw in the mirror; the big pointed ears and the scraggled hair. The unease in the eyes which stared back at her so shiftily.

I am finished, Annie said to herself. Before long I will die and they will cart me off to the graveyard. But before that happens I will go crazy. I do not have any future; it is all finished. I wish I could tell the future or knew somebody that did. If I could find somebody that could say the future, could say that it was going to be this way or that way, then I'd know. And then I'd stop worrying.

The days and the fact that nobody seemed to be noticing what was happening to her ground on her nerves. She sat at the piano and practiced her recital piece and on purpose hit some wrong notes and Ruth, in another part of the house, yelled, "That isn't right! You know it isn't! Go back and do it over now and do it right this time!"

Her feet on the piano pedals felt hot and huge. She

looked down at them and slid to the far end of the bench. She let her hands hang limply between her knees and hunched her shoulders. She closed her eyes and felt the time clicking by. Always it was going to be this way. She would grow old and crazy sitting here in this house with Ruth and Calvin and her father. Her head felt queerly light; she could feel the sluggish blood in it sloshing around. Like the weather, her blood was hot and sticky.

In her father's bedroom-office Calvin was pecking at the typewriter and the neighborhood children were shrieking in the street outside and in the kitchen Ruth was singing her loud, vulgar songs. And in other parts of the town the baboons and the mules were talking about her—were saying that now that she was old enough she was going to be just like Norma.

With her fist Annie banged on the piano keyboard six times, and the typewriter pecking in her father's office-bedroom hesitated and went on and Ruth appeared. She said, "You think you're going to beat Shack Vareen come recital time? Playing the way you've been playing this morning? You'll never do it. I went by the Vareens' house last night on my way home and I heard Shack practicing and it was like angel music. All the neighbors were listening, that's how pretty it was. Shack hits every note just right."

"Let her," said Annie. "I don't care. I got other things on my mind."

Ruth polished the top of the television set with the hem of her skirt. "Like what, for instance?"

"Like," said Annie, "they're saying that now I'm old enough I'm going to be just like Norma."

"Who is they?"

"Everybody. Suedella Jackson and Gwendolyn Ross."

Ruth went around the room wiping dust with the hem of her skirt. "You should tell your daddy; he'd fix it. He'd shut them up quick."

"No."

Ruth was looking at her. "Why not?"

The reason escaped her. It had to do with the process of being nice, the way her father wanted her to be. And it had to do with her sometimes-anger toward him and her pride of him. He was a pharmacist—the very next thing to being a doctor—and the people in the town respected him. They would respect him less if he, like some common person, went around punching people in the nose. They would punch him back and somebody would go to jail and afterward have to appear before Judge Jackson in court. It was too common. It was not for her father.

So she said, "I don't know why not. Quit pestering me with that question. I'm just saying that's what they're saying about me. I'm just saying I know how Calvin got here. I know what made him."

Ruth was plumping the davenport pillows, mixing the orange tasseled ones with the plain black ones. With this problem she was being stealthy and secret because she didn't know the answer to it. She was punching the pillows harder than they needed to be punched and little puffs of dust and lint were coming from them. She said, "Well, I never lied to you about him. I never told you the stork brought him or the doctor jerked him down from heaven."

"You never told me anything," said Annie. "But I know. Suedella told me all about how a thing like this happens the last time I was over to her house. It's a disgrace. I think the least Norma could have done was to marry Calvin's father. The way it is now we're a disgrace in this town."

Ruth was down on her hands and knees examining a spot on the carpet. It had been there a long time; she would never do anything about it. Still, she examined it as if its presence was new and as if she intended to do something about it right away. "Norma didn't want to marry Calvin's father. You've got to get that through your head. I don't know why you can't. To me it's simple. She had already made one mistake and she didn't want to make another. I should think that'd be simple enough for anybody to understand."

Annie leered at Ruth. "Well, where is Calvin's father now? You never think to tell me anything unless I outright ask you. Where is he? Does he live here in this town? If he does he should be ashamed of himself."

Ruth's candle-white smile was sad and patient. "Honey, he doesn't live here any more. Neither does his family. They moved up north years and years ago. Now I don't know why you're thinking along the lines you're thinking. These are modern times. You see your daddy's car; it's no Model T. And you see our nice, big refrigerator that spits its own ice cubes and defrosts itself. And our color television set. Men have already landed on the moon. All these things are modern things in these modern times. I just can't understand why you have to think old-fashioned with all these modern things around you. All this stuff about Calvin ruining your reputation is just plain foolishness. Nobody thinks about stuff like that any more. People have liberated themselves from all that old-fashioned thinking. That's what you should do. You should just liberate yourself from it and go on and be the sweet little girl you can be sometimes and have a good time. If you can't do that I don't know what to tell you to do."

Annie patted her knees and her face. "I wish I could say the future or find somebody else that could. I wish I could find out what's going to happen to me; what I'm going to be. If I don't find it out I will go crazy. I will do something bad I won't be responsible for."

Ruth had risen. She stood looking at Annie and there was a queer debate going on in her eyes. "People go crazy from diseases; not from just saying they will. Are you through practicing?"

"Yes."

"You going to work on your book now?"

"No."

"Why not?"

"I hate it. I am going crazy. But before that happens I am going to have Suedella Jackson and Gwendolyn arrested. I am going to have them put in jail for calling Calvin what they did. And for saying that now I'm old enough I'm going to be just like Norma."

Ruth came to the piano and closed the black hood over the keyboard. She went around in back of the davenport and picked up a sandal that belonged to Calvin. "I know a woman who can say the future. Before I went to Charleston summer before last—you remember that?—she predicted I'd go. She predicted the whole thing. She said in Jacksonville a nice man would buy me my dinner and that's what happened. She said he'd be wearing a red ring and he was. She said we'd eat fried shrimp in a cafeteria and we did. She said before we got to Charleston on the bus he'd ask me to marry him and he did."

Annie lifted her head to look at Ruth. "You never told me anybody asked you to marry him on that trip."

"I didn't want you to worry," explained Ruth. "But it happened. And it was all predicted by this woman I'm telling you about; the one who can say of the future."

Annie fingered the stubs of her hair and rubbed the soles of her feet together. She didn't altogether believe Ruth. This story of hers concerning the Charleston trip sounded slippery, as if the details of it had been manufactured to suit the demands of the occasion. Still, it was possible. And Ruth never lied.

She rubbed the shin of her left leg with her right foot. The shin had a round scar on it, a holdover from her tree climbing days. "What is this woman's name?" she asked.

The answer shot out of Ruth's mouth. "Madame Cecile. If you think you're really interested in having her say your future I could have her come here tonight right after supper. I could phone her now and make the appointment."

"How much does she charge?"

"A dollar for bad news and two dollars for good," answered Ruth.

"Make an appointment," said Annie. "Tell her to come tonight. Right after supper. Don't tell my father about this; I don't want him to know about it. If it's bad news I *sure* don't want him to know about it."

"I hear you," said Ruth and trotted to the telephone.

The pecking of the typewriter in her father's room was constant. Annie went to the door of the room and stood, with her head slightly averted, watched Calvin from the corner of her eye. To make the chair at the typing table right for him he had brought in a pile of books. Dressed in red shorts and red tee shirt and his bush hat he was perched on top of the books. He was pleased with what he was doing. Every once in a while, in the middle of typing a word, he would stop and smile to himself.

After a minute or two Annie went into the room and walked around and around the typing table. She forced herself to look at Calvin. "What are you typing?"

Under the bush hat Calvin's head bobbed. He struck a wrong key and he gazed at it in momentary dismay. He smiled. "My book."

"What's it about?"

"Flowers."

"Flowers," said Annie. "I might've known it. I might've known you'd pick a sissy subject like that."

Calvin's little hands rested on the keyboard of the typewriter. "I like flowers," he whispered. "They're so pretty and they smell so nice. If I wasn't what I am I'd like to be a flower. A sweet pea if I could have my pick. If you could be a flower what kind would you be, Annie?"

"Flowers are silly," said Annie. "I wouldn't be one."

Calvin pushed his hat back and his green eyes solemnly regarded her. "Flowers aren't silly. They're nice. Everybody likes them."

Crazily, Annie felt the blood in her head splash. It went in a hot, forceful wave to the front of her head and then drained backwards. She walked around and around the typing table and Calvin's eyes followed her. She thought of what she would like to be if she wasn't in her present form and could have her pick. Something that would offend—something bitter. "I would like," she said, "to be a turnip. I would rather be a turnip than anything. A big, bitter turnip that'd make people gag when they ate me. All the mules and the baboons. They'd boil me and my leaves and I'd stink up their houses. They'd put sugar in me to make me sweet but I'd still be bitter."

Calvin shuddered. "No. I wouldn't like to be anything that was to eat. Least of all a turnip." He lifted his hat from his head and fanned his face with it. "Let's go to the library, Annie." He picked and pecked at her until finally she allowed herself to be persuaded though the last thing she wanted to do was to walk into town with Calvin at her side; the library had always been a place of just lukewarm interest to her. Still she allowed herself to be persuaded.

In the dry, searing heat Annie and Calvin went to town. They went through the two vacant lots that were puckered brown from the sun and she walked normally so that Calvin did not have to run to keep up with her. The brittle grasses beneath their feet crackled with each step and the sun over them was a great, molten bulb but they didn't speak of the heat or their thirst.

They came to the sidewalk that led into the town and stepped out on it and went past Professor Evans's music studio and then The Gray Moss Inn and the old people on the porch of it woke from their dozings to lean and look at them. They sucked their mouths and their whisperings were like the twitterings of old, tattered birds.

"What were they saying?" asked Calvin from under his hat.

Annie turned and made a quick, ugly face to the company of the porch. "They weren't saying anything," she answered. "They're just old birds with their brains worn out. That's what this whole town is full of; old birds with their brains worn out and baboons and mules. I wouldn't give you a nickle with a hole punched in it for all of them."

This new, contemptuous philosophy of hers overcame all externals. She didn't feel the heat on her head or the thirst in her throat. Calvin wanted to stop at Jelks' Drugstore for a cold drink but she said, "No, we'll stop on the way back. Right now we're going to the library. I've heard you yap about it until I'm sick of it. We're going to the library and you're going to look at every book in it even if it takes four hours."

The library was old and gloomy and cool and smelled of old, moth-scented coverings and new, slick ones. Its hushed atmosphere was solitary. There was a vase of faded roses on the entrance desk and there was Miss Velda Dishman behind the desk.

Annie and Calvin stood in front of the desk and Miss Dishman looked up at them and Calvin's grin was ecstatic. "Want to look at your books," he whispered. "All of them." He had removed his hat and his white head glinted like tinsel in the strong light streaming in through the bare windows.

Miss Dishman smiled at Calvin and gave him permission to look at the books and he tiptoed away from the desk to the first aisle and knelt there. He clasped his hands over his stomach and gazed in rapture at the books and in a minute selected one, opened it, and was immediately lost.

Annie continued to stand at the desk, smelling the faded roses in the vase and looking at Miss Dishman who was leafing through a catalog and making notes on a separate sheet. The backs of her hands were peppered with little brown spots and her scalp, shining pinkly through the puffs of her silver hair, looked clean and smooth.

Annie reflected that Miss Dishman must be at least fifty years old—an incredible age.

Annie stood first on one foot and then another. Her feet hurt her; she could feel them growing. The atmosphere in this place was queer; it seemed so far removed from real, earthly things. After a minute she said, "You've sure got a lot of books in here. I never noticed before how many. It's kind of crazy when you stop to think of it."

Miss Dishman lifted her eyes. "Crazy?"

"I mean queer. It's kind of queer, all these books in here. I never noticed before how many."

Miss Dishman closed her catalog. "Well, there is a first time for everything."

Annie locked her knees and fingered her hair. "Books've never interested me much although I'm writing one in my spare time."

"I know," said Miss Dishman. "Your father told me."

"It smells funny in here," said Annie.

Miss Dishman's fragile hands were taking the wilted roses from the vase; she was rolling them in a piece of newspaper and placing them in the wastebasket. "That's because you're not accustomed to the odor of books. Actually what you smell is not an odor; it's a scent."

"It just smells odd," murmured Annie. "That's all I meant to say."

"I love it," said Miss Dishman. "If I couldn't smell books and be with them every day I would die."

Calvin had seated himself on the floor in the aisle nearest the desk. He had pulled four thick volumes from the shelves and had stacked these in a pile beside him. He stood up, squinting at the shelves and reaching for more.

"He'll want to take them all home," said Annie. "He loves books."

"He's beautiful," said Miss Dishman simply. "One day he will rule the world."

Annie laughed.

"His kind will," said Miss Dishman, unperturbed. "They always have."

Annie swallowed what was left of her laugh. Miss Dishman wasn't being funny. She was being serious and she was believing in what she said. Her blue, blue eyes were calmly, darkly shining and now there was strength in the set of her jaw. She was looking at Calvin as if she had known him forever, and as if she loved him. "He has discovered books," she said. "The world will never beat him. It will never even hurt him very much. He will conquer the world."

In imitation of Calvin, Annie folded her hands across her stomach. She wanted to challenge Miss Dishman's opinion but there was something too certain in it; it had the ring of the biggest truth she had ever heard. It was very, very queer. "How?" she asked. "How will Calvin conquer the world with just books?"

Miss Dishman was taking books from her desk and

73

stacking them into a grocery cart that she had drawn alongside the desk. There came her answer. "His mind," she said. "His mind will do it. The books will give him the power to do it."

Annie stood patting her ears and pulling at the ends of her hair. She had a sudden vision of what *she* could do with just a little power. Impossible things that concerned the mules and the baboons of the town. She could bring them to their knees and make them beg for her forgiveness. She could make them wish they had never heard of her or laid eyes on her. She could put Suedella Jackson and Gwendolyn Ross in jail and keep them there until they became crones.

Miss Dishman was pushing the cart with its load of books away from the desk. She was moving toward the center aisle of the room.

Annie went after her. "About this power from books," she said. "Maybe I've been missing out on something. Maybe I should really go after it. You think I should?"

It was evening and Madame Cecile had come to say Annie's future. Annie had forgotten about Madame Cecile. She had a new, absorbing interest, one that was taking all of her time and energy and now Ruth could not argue her from her room.

"You'll just have to tell Madame Cecile to come back some other time," Annie said. "I don't have time to hear my future now. Tell her to say yours if she's so cracked on saying somebody's. I'll pay for it."

"You and Calvin are both going to go blind," predicted Ruth. "All these books. You didn't even eat your supper."

"What does diffident mean?" asked Annie frowning down at her book.

Ruth confessed to her ignorance of the word and crept away.

Annie went to Calvin's room and consulted his dictionary.

CHAPTER FIVE

THE POWER in the books she lugged home from the library eluded her. It was maddening to always have to stop and look up the meanings of words in the dictionary. It seemed to her that the authors of the books had deliberately set out to mystify her and harass her. The books exhausted and frustrated her. She would sit in her father's office-bedroom with Calvin and for long periods there would be only the sound of pages turning and the soft creakings from Calvin's rocker and her own sighs. Occasionally she would become engrossed in some clearly stated passage and would fall under the silent influence of the book in her hand. It would be rather pleasant sitting there in the fan-cooled room with Calvin, sipping iced drinks, reading about the relics of ancient eras and the glories of modern times. But then she would come to a paragraph containing whole strings of unknown words and she would throw the book across the room and bitterly declare that she was done. "It's dumb," she would say. "It's the dumbest thing I ever got mixed up in. They want people to read their dumb old books but they don't write them so's anybody who

wants to read them can understand them. These books
. . . these books, they're just plain goading. The whole
thing goads me. I am through with it and if you don't
think so you are just plain pragmatical."

Calvin laid aside his own book. He raised his arm to
his mouth and thoughtfully licked the inside of it.
"What's pragmatical?"

"Questions. Questions, questions all day long. I wish
I was deaf."

"Well, you're the one who said it. I didn't. You're
the one who said it and now you should tell me what
it means. What's pragmatical?"

"Pragmatical means meddlesome, Calvin. It means
self-important. You should look up words you don't
know like I do. It's no fun for me to have to sit in here
explaining words to you all day long. If you think it is
you've got an idiosyncrasy of some kind or another."

Calvin lowered his arm. His eyes strayed toward the
dictionary resting on the little table in the corner of
the room. "I can't spell as good as you," he whispered.
"And Ruth can't either. I can't look up words if I
don't know how to spell them. It's awful."

There was a sudden feeling of strain in the room.
The world was outside and it was doing things. Its
oceans were rocking and its volcanoes were erupting
and its plains and stones were being explored and examined. All over the world there was movement—interesting people doing interesting things. They were calling each other up on the telephone and going to little
dress-up parties and watermelon cuttings and going to

77

matinees at the Ritz Theater. Yet here she sat in this stuffy room with Calvin and all they could think to talk about was words. What good was it all if the world outside was going to leave her behind? Miss Dishman was a liar. There wasn't any power in books. All they did was make you mad—make you realize how ignorant you were.

Calvin had left his chair to go to the typing table. He was pushing her papers around, getting them all mixed up. His glasses had slipped down onto the bridge of his nose and he was humming. He lifted a sheet of paper from the pile at his elbow and inserted it in the typewriter. "I'm going to write a letter to my mother," he announced.

Abruptly Annie was reminded of what Suedella had called Calvin and what her former friends expected of her—to be like Norma. She closed her eyes and felt the pulse in her brain beat against her skull. She was Annie Jelks and there wasn't any power on earth that could change that. Forever things were going to be as they were now. She would grow old and gray and toothless sitting here in this room with Calvin learning words and reading books and the power that was in them would never be revealed to her because there wasn't any. Miss Dishman was an old fool baboon and a liar.

Calvin was kneeling on the chair at the typing table. He was smiling at his blank sheet of paper. "I'm going to tell my mother about the flower book I'm writing," he said.

Annie opened her eyes and looked at her nephew

and was siezed with anger toward him and what had made him. Her own inertia in this scheme of things that worked against her was suddenly infuriating. "Get away from that typewriter," she said. "I want to use it now."

Calvin pulled his sheet of paper from the machine. Holding it in his hand, he slid down from the chair and went toward the rocker. He sat down in it and picked up his book. In a minute he was engrossed in his reading.

Annie rose and went to the typing table. "I've got a new idea for a book," she lied. "And I want to write it down before I forget it. You can write to your mother later when I'm finished."

Calvin was silent. He rocked and kept his eyes glued to the pages of his book.

"That other one I started wasn't any good," she said. "It came to me too quick and I didn't use the right words. This one's going to be different. But first I have to think of what name I'm going to write under. It can't be my real one. I hate my name; it's so common. I've been thinking about Catherine R. Kingston. The R is for Rene or Rosalind, I can't make up my mind which."

Calvin stilled the squeakings of his rocker. He closed his book and clasped it to his chest. He considered. After a minute he said, "I think Annie Jelks is pretty. It's the prettiest name I ever heard. I don't like Catherine R. Kingston. It doesn't make me think of you."

Annie sat with her face cupped in her hands and

stared at the typewriter. She should write about people and she shouldn't have them sweet like Cordelia, her queen. She should make people in her book real and interesting. It should be about a judge's daughter and her name should be Maude. Maude had a disease that had emaciated her to the point of looking farcical and she deserved it though she was only a little over twelve. Maude had skeletons hanging in her closet. She was a vampire, that's what her disease was. She lived by sucking the blood out of other people's bodies, stealing into their houses at night when they were asleep. Before her disease Maude had been a gorgeous woman of infamous character and all the men in town had been after her but then one day she had a little child and this child was so uncomely that she couldn't bear to look at it and stuffed it in the wastebasket where it died and after that Maude lost her mind. Now she was a vampire and only came out of her house at night and everybody in town was terrified silly of her. No, not everybody. There was one girl in town who wasn't. This girl was a famous authoress and she knew about vampires. Well, so one night Maude went to this girl's room to suck her blood and the girl leaped up out of her bed and drove a stake through Maude's heart which is the only way to kill vampires. And then this girl wrote a book about Maude and it was made into a movie. Now she was rich and went to Paris—the real Paris—to buy her clothes. She only took her old servant with her. They flew. On a plane.

It took Annie until suppertime to write this story. She was pleased with it. Calvin teased her to tell him what it was about but she wouldn't.

After the evening meal Ruth went home and Calvin wanted to be entertained and she showed him how to write secret messages in lemon juice:

IN THE MORASS
THERE LIVES A JACKASS.
HER INITIALS ARE S. J.

Over heat this message turned a deep, revealing mustard color and Calvin was fascinated. He squeezed two more lemons, printed his name on a separate sheet of paper, watched the letters turn brown, voiced his intention to keep it forever.

She played her recital piece for him and he yawned and went to bed.

In the yard there were long, hulking shadows under the trees and along the fence line. She went outside and walked around in the cool grass. Near the goldfish pond a bullfrog hiccoughed, *Ku-yuk, ku-yuk,* and the white stars in the sky seemed big and close. She wanted her father to come home and sit and talk with her.

When he came he was tired and irritable. She showed him her vampire story and after he had read the pages he looked at her in disgust.

"You don't like it," she asked.

Her father shook his head. "No."

"But I spent practically all day on it," she protested. "And I used all my new words. What don't you like about it?"

Her father was removing his shoes. There was some white powdered stuff on the tip of one and he rubbed it away with his palm. "Maude," he said. "That's what I don't like about it."

"You don't like Maude? Well, why not for curse's sake?"

"A human vampire. Where did you get such a weird notion anyway?"

"I saw it in an old movie."

Her father set both of his shoes on the floor. "And the business about Maude having a baby and stuffing it in the wastebasket."

"You didn't like that part? I did. That's where it belonged, don't you see? In the wastebasket. Or in an orphanage. You don't understand it, that's what's wrong. All right, I'll fix it. I'll take the vampire out. Nobody believes in them any more anyway except some Slavonic people. Miss Dishman told me that. But the part about the baby I can't do anything about. It—"

"Maybe," suggested her father, "the baby had grand-parents. In that case they would have wanted it no matter how ugly it was."

Annie shook her head. "No. There weren't any. And even if there had've been they wouldn't have wanted it. It was a disgrace. Don't you see that?"

Her father was looking at her steadily and solemnly and now the innocent, simple business of discussing her story had become a trap. It had slipped beyond her control. There was dry silence in the room and her father's eyes were boring into hers. She patted the tips of her ears and rubbed the soles of her bare feet together. "But it's just a story," she said. "I don't want to argue with anybody about it."

Her father continued to look at her.

She put her feet flat on the floor. They were growing again. She could feel the expanding ache in the toes and heels of them. The pain in them made her eyes water. She said, "I know what you're thinking but you just don't need to. Everybody in my story was made up. Especially the baby. Well, maybe Maude is a little bit like Suedella Jackson. I admit that. But the rest of them are completely made up. Especially the baby."

Her father was sitting forward in his chair. The light was on his head and for the first time she noticed the gray in his hair. He said, "The baby in your story is the most important character, isn't he?"

"The most important character? No, I don't think so. He's just there. He died."

"Were you glad when he died?"

"Glad? I don't know what you mean. *I* didn't put him in the wastebasket. Maude did. All the people in town were talking about him, calling him names—"

"What names?"

"Names. I don't know what ones. And Maude—"

"I want to know what names, Annie. I want you to tell me what names."

The clock on the wall was striking. It chimed eleven

times and the two in the room continued to sit, looking at each other. This was the night for first things—for the aging in her father to be noticed by Annie for the first time and for a fear of him to be felt for the first time. It had never happened before. She twisted around in her chair and pressed her fingertips to her temples.

Her father wasn't going to give up. He was leaning forward, forcing her to look at him. He said, "I want to know what names the people in your town were calling the baby, Annie."

She let her hands drop from her head. She put them between her knees, letting them dangle. "Now I can't remember," she said. "Anyway, it doesn't make any difference now. Nobody believes in vampires any more and the baby—"

"I want to know what names they were calling him, Annie."

"I can't say it," she whispered.

"Why not?"

"God might strike me dead."

"I can almost guarantee," declared her father, "that He won't. What names were the people in your story calling the baby? Tell me."

"No."

Her father said the word oh, so gently. "Is that the one?" he asked. "Is that the word your friends called Calvin?"

She clenched her fists and bit her lips.

"We'll stay here all night," said her father. "We'll

stay here until you tell me. Is that the word your friends called Calvin?"

"Yes!" she cried. "Yes! Yes! Suedella Jackson called him that and I told her I was going to have her arrested and put in jail and she said I couldn't because that's what he was and I know it's the truth and I wish I was dead! I don't know what you were thinking about letting him come here to live with us! You knew it would make me suffer! Oh, if I had some money I'd leave here tomorrow and go so far away you'd never hear from me again!"

Her father's face never lost its composure. He reached in his pocket and withdrew his wallet. He pulled money from it, leaned, and laid it on the table at her elbow. He picked up his shoes and went to his room and closed the door.

The house was so quiet. After a while the clock on the wall chimed midnight.

The bullfrog in the yard hiccoughed all night: *Ku-yuk, ku-yuk, ku-yuk.*

It was six o'clock in the morning and out of all the people in the town she was the only one awake. The houses in her neighborhood stood in the gray silence with their night shades drawn and nothing behind them stirred or made a sound. Their blank, rigid fronts looked blankly out to the empty street.

Annie took one final look at the front of her own house and then the back of it. Light sprawled in shapeless patterns on the lawn. The bullfrog had finally gone someplace else to do his croaking; a spider had spun a silver web in the Turk's-cap lily at the corner of the house. A shoe that belonged to Calvin lay lopsided on the lowest step of the porch. Annie sniffed and turned away. The suitcase in her hand bumped against her knees. She crossed the yard and left it and didn't look back.

She was on her way to town to catch the first bus to anywhere. During the night she had had time to consider a destination but hadn't settled on one. The money her father had laid out for her travel wasn't enough to take her to Paris, France, or even to snow country. She would just have to wait and see how far it *would* take her. When she got to where she was going she would get a job in a drugstore. She would rent a room close by and change her name to Catherine Rosalind Kingston and on Sundays she would go to church and no one would question her right to be there. She would never allow herself to be in love; she would never have any children. She would just work in a drugstore someplace and live alone and be quietly happy. As of right this minute she was no longer Annie Jelks, aunt to Calvin Jelks and sister to Norma Jelks. She was Catherine Rosalind Kingston and she was all alone in the world. Attired in her black and white executive dress and the black shoes that hurt her feet, Annie hurried through the vacant lots.

The sun was coming up; through the tangle of tall

trees on the eastern boundary of the lots its rays shone clear red. It was going to be a long, hot day.

Annie sat on a bench in front of the bus station and waited for the man who operated the station to arrive. She suspected a blister on one of her heels and a quick examination confirmed the suspicion. The walk to town in the stiff shoes had rubbed her heel raw. She took a tissue from her purse, tore a square from it and applied it to the wound. She sat on the bench making vague plans, watching the sun slipping down over the tops of the building and into the unpeopled street and presently the bus station operator arrived. He was disheveled and in a hurry. As he rushed past her to the doors of the station she smelled his unwashed odor. He fumbled with his keys and pushed the doors open.

From her bench Annie peered through the large window and watched this man ready the station for the day's business. In a minute she picked up her suitcase and went inside. She approached the ticket window and the station operator, busy with stacks of wrinkled paper, looked up at her.

"I want to go someplace," Annie said, "but I haven't quite decided where. I thought you might make a suggestion to me."

The man's square, stained hands continued to organize his papers. "Suggestions are a little out of my line. Most people comin' in here know where they want to go. You running away from home or somethin'?"

Annie sat her purse on the counter. "Don't be silly.

Of course I'm not running away from home. My father knows I'm going; he gave me the money to. I want to go to a city, I think. What time does your next bus go to a city and what's the name of it?"

This man really did smell; there was no question about it. His collar, where it had rubbed against the back of his neck, was dark-greasy and he had loose dandruff and he wasn't interested in her. "I got a bus going to Ocala in ten minutes," he said.

Annie bought a ticket to Ocala. She chose a seat in the center of the bus and as it bore her out of town, past the Ritz Theater and Jelks' Drugstore, past the A&P and Pratney's Funeral Home and then through the sad section of the town where Ruth lived, she occupied herself with her heel blister. She eased the shoe from her wounded foot and with the greatest of care peeled back the tissue bandage. Some skin came with it and the pain of this brought the tears to her eyes.

The bus left the town and with a gathering of its machinery sped out on the open highway. The road took them through scrub country where the sand was white and the land peppered thick with scrub vegetation—spindly sand pines and dog fennel and bear grass. Ragged fences were no barrier for wandering cattle. Gently decayed, wild homes appeared at unexpected times along the bumpy, winding trail. Red and yellow trumpet vines grew around their sagging doors and the immense magnolia trees shading them rattled their glossy leaves in the warm wind.

The bus went fast and Annie sat alone in the center

of it, nursing her sore heel and making anxious plans. There were other passengers—a sallow man with a bright, raised scar on his cheek, a black family of six who sat silently, a white woman with a child who cried sickishly. None of these spoke to her. After a time the sick child slept and the sallow man went forward to speak to the bus driver.

It wasn't a long trip and at the end of it Annie experienced disappointment for Ocala was no city, not like Jacksonville or Atlanta. She stood on a corner across the street from the bus station looking in at the windows of the shops, looking for a rooming house and a drugstore. She found the drugstore and went into it and sat on a stool at the fountain. Shrewdly she ordered a Cherry Smash. The boy in back of the fountain shook his head and waited for her to change her order.

"But a Cherry Smash is so simple," she said. "I've made a million of them in my drugstore. Back where I come from I'm famous for them; I invented them. Silver Nip too; I invented Silver Nip. Back in my town everybody drinks Cherry Smash and Silver Nip. Look, you're missing out on something real good if you don't know how to make these two simple drinks. I could show you how in just a minute. Want me to? Say, you don't need another soda jerk around here, do you? You see I just arrived on the bus and I—"

"You want a Coke?" asked the boy.

Annie glared at him. "No. You're rude, did anybody ever tell you that? Dumb too. I think I should speak to the manager about you. Where is he?"

The boy grinned at her. "I'm the manager's son. You got a complaint, give it to me. I'll see he gets it."

No drugstore in Ocala wanted to hire her. She couldn't persuade them to her way of thinking. Neither could she find a room to rent. The rooming-house people were suspicious of her. They didn't believe her when she said she was eighteen and only wanted a room for the innocent purpose of living in it. They didn't believe that she was Catherine Rosalind Kingston.

At two o'clock in the afternoon Annie Jelks sat in the public library pretending an interest in the books spread open on the table before her. She was there because the library was the safest, friendliest place she could think of. She needed this quiet hour to collect herself and make new plans, for she was footsore and heartsick and now more than just a little afraid. She was friendless, completely so, and she had no weapons with which to combat this frail, wretched condition. She was a victim, that's what she was. Sister of Norma Jelks and aunt of Calvin Jelks and if she gave up now and went back to her home town that's what she'd always be. Forever she would be watched and whispered about and shunned and Norma, who was the cause of the whole thing, would go her own cool way out in California and nothing bad was ever going to happen to Calvin. She herself didn't have the stomach to do away with him; that much had been proved. And he was never going to get a disease that would kill him. Ruth and her father would see to that. They would protect him with their lives if necessary. Smart little wart. Little pug-ugly nuisance. Little show-off with his dumb flower book and his big vocabulary.

The library was a little dark, a little gloomy because outside the sun had gone. There was dark rain and the rumble of summer thunder. The rain beat against the windows and no one thought to come in and turn on any lights and the odors from the shelves were dry and strange.

Sitting alone in this room Annie sniffed and absently turned a page in one of her books. Her eyes smarted and she dug her fists in them and rubbed. The tears came. I am sick, she thought. This time I really am. And nobody knows I'm here. It would serve them right if I just sat here with these fool books and expired. Expired? Where'd that word come from? Probably from that little baboon Calvin. Lately her brain had developed a trick of storing up his nitwitted words, popping them out at her when she wasn't looking.

With a used tissue Annie wiped her dirty tears away and set her jaw. She couldn't go out into the street again squalling; people would think she was bloogers. The rain was beating a sharp tattoo against the windows and the thunder was directly over the building.

Annie pulled one of the books toward her and applied herself to the business of reading a philosophy not immediately comprehended: *Truly each new book is as a ship that bears us away from the fixity of our limitations into the movement and splendor of life's infinite ocean.* The words had been written by Helen Keller, the most famous, blind deaf-mute in American history.

Frowning, Annie slid way back in her chair but immediately slid forward to the edge of it again to re-read. *The fixity of our limitations.* What did that mean? It was something . . . something that had to do with her personally. She felt this. She knew it. But what? *The fixity of our limitations.* Oh, curses, it was a pain to be such a numbskull.

Annie sighed and twisted around in her chair, avoiding the sight of the big dictionary on the stand beneath the windows but in a minute she rose and hobbled over to it and angrily sought the meaning of the words *fixity* and *limitations.*

In the green dusk Annie went home. When she stood on the front porch of her house all of the sun had withdrawn from the sky and the heat was cooling away. She stood up close to the screen door and listened. Ruth and Calvin were in the kitchen having supper and they were being very quiet about this. They were talking about the food they were eating, whether their fish cakes should have had more onion in them, whether the biscuits had been overbaked, whether they should have whipped cream or ice cream on their peach pie. They were talking about their supper food as if it was the most important thing in the whole world.

Without a sound Annie set her suitcase down. She leaned against the screen door and breathed deeply. The odors of home assailed her; flowering jasmine, fish cakes, peach pie, and Ruth's chicory coffee. Things were so quiet but restless, too. In a bog of reeds far down at the furthermost perimeter of the vacant lots where few besides herself had ever ventured, jack-o'-lanterns glowed, the light from them mysteriously rising and falling with every breath of the wind. A chuck-will's-widow called and there was something in this profound and vaguely troubling.

Annie opened the screen door and stepped inside the house. She swaggered back to the kitchen and Ruth and Calvin turned from the table to look at her.

Annie said, "Hey. I see I'm just in time for supper."

With a precise gesture Ruth set her pie fork crosswise on her plate. "Where have you been? Your daddy's got the whole police force out looking for you. He's with them. Now just where have you been?"

Annie sat at the table and helped herself to a piece of warm peach pie. Calvin was staring at her; she ignored him. "I was in Ocala," she said. "The man at the bus station could've told you that if you had thought to ask him."

Ruth rolled her eyes. "We asked. But the man who was there this morning took off at noon and went fishing. What's the big idea? Just answer me that if it isn't too much trouble. Oh, you just wait till your daddy gets home! He'll phone again in a minute. You just wait till he does! This time you're really going to catch it, Miss Priss-Prass! You just wait and see!"

Annie finished her first piece of pie and helped herself to another.

"It's better with ice cream," whispered Calvin. "Here. Take mine. I don't want it."

With her fork Annie smoothed the ice cream over the crust of the pie. "I found out something important today," she said. "That's why I'm back. I found out about the fixity of my limitations and what to do about them. Does anybody here know what that means? Does anybody here know how important that is?"

Ruth was applying herself to her own pie and ice cream. "No, I don't know what any fixity of limitations means and I'm not interested in finding out. Is pie all you're going to eat? You'd better take my advice and fortify yourself with something a little more solid. I think you're going to need it."

"I am," said Annie, "going to take a trip on a ship. It will bear me away from the fixity of my limitations into the movement and splendor of life's infinite ocean."

The phone was ringing and Ruth was getting up to go and answer it. The sound of her voice, loud and jubilant and nervous, filled the house. "She's back, Mr. Jelks! You better come home now. Where was she all day? Well, Mr. Jelks, she was in Ocala finding out about something called the fixity of her limitations. I think there's something wrong with her .No, not physical. Mental. Just now she said to me that she was going to take a trip on a ship that would bear her away from the fixity of her limitations into the movement and splendor of life's infinite ocean. That sounds sick to me. Doesn't it to you?"

At the table in the kitchen Annie finished her pie and wiped her mouth with Ruth's discarded napkin. Across from her Calvin was sitting perfectly still. His lips were composed and his great, green eyes resting on her were sharply alight. They shared with her the pleasure of this new turn of possibility.

CHAPTER SIX

SO THAT THE whole town could observe her journey
away from the fixity of her limitations and into the
splendor of life's infinite ocean Annie moved the typing
table and the typewriter from the house to the front
yard. She made herself a little office under the shade
of the oak trees. She set Calvin's dictionary on an up-
ended concrete block and established a card table, containing a pencil caddy, a pile of yellow paper, a stack
of library books, a pitcher of ice water, and two paper
cups, nearby. Calvin bore his rocker from the house
and set it close to the card table. Clutching a book of
his own he helped himself to a cup of water, sat down,
adjusted his spectacles and gazed at her. "I can't find
my other pair of glasses," he said. "I think they're lost.
Anyway I think they'd be too small for your head.
Anyway, I don't think they'd do you any good. They
were made especially for me because I have myopia.
I've got a suggestion to make though. Bryant Cape—
you remember him? The man who used to cook spaghetti for my mother and me? Well, I can tell you what
he used to do when *he* wanted to make people think

he was smarter than he was. He had a pair of plainos, see."

"A pair of what, Calvin?"

"Plainos. They're specs like these I wear but with just plain glass in them. A lot of people in Hollywood wear them when they want to look older and smarter then they are. Bryant Cape did. They don't cost very much. Coupla dollars maybe. Probably you could get a pair at the ten-cent store. But I honestly don't see why you want them. You look smart and old just like you are."

In her judgment the plainos, which cost $1.98 at the five-and-dime store, made her look cunningly professional. They made her look literary. Seated at the table under the oak trees, she lolled her feet and fingered her hair and considered the subject of the book she was about to start writing. The heroine in it was going to be twelve years old or so. Miss Dishman had advised this. So to get the juices in her mind started she had read eighteen books concerning girls twelve years old or so. All of them had disgusted her; they were so dull and unreal. They had just sickened her with their sweetness and do-goodness and fairly-tale pabulum. The heroines in all of them had been pretty and virtuous. None had ever told a lie, hated anybody, cheated at anything, looked at anything they weren't supposed to look at or listened to anything they weren't supposed to hear. They cried every time anybody even looked at them cross-eyed but did this bravely, in secret. In these books people with fatal illnesses always recovered

in time for Christmas and criminals were always persuaded by the heroines to turn pure.

These books weren't honest but hers was going to be.
It was going to be artistic, too, more artistic than entrepreneurial. Entrepreneurial? Curses. Out of what layer
of her mind had *that* word come from and what did it
mean? Probably she had heard it from that old baboon
Miss Dishman who loved to use words people didn't
know the meanings of just to torment them. Entrepreneurial. Rats. Anybody who used a word that big should
be shot.

Annie sighed and glanced at Calvin. Placidly rocking, he was engrossed in his own book. Under his bush
hat his head was nodding agreement with what he was
reading. Annie left her chair and went to the dictionary.
The word *entrepreneurial* exhausted her because, in the
pursuit of its meaning, she became lost in others: entre-
nous and entrepôt and entresol. Entresol made her stomach squinch. She slammed the dictionary shut and went
back to her chair. An affliction she hadn't known she
possessed appeared—great, itchy, nervous bumps, one
on each cheek and two on her neck.

Curiously and sympathetically Calvin was looking
at her. "You've got nervous bumps," he observed.
"They're white in the centers. Don't think about words
for a minute and they'll go away."

In the backroads of her mind the ghost of an idea
had started to brew. In an effort to help it materialize
she sat very still and more nervous bumps came. A
green chameleon fell from an overhead branch to the

back of her hand and immediately turned the same color as her skin. It seemed unafraid and not in any hurry to leave. She looked down at it, curiously noting its short head ornamented with dermal flaps and its large eye, enclosed by fused eyelids except for a small central opening.

"It won't bite you," said Calvin, rising from his rocker to look. "I've got a book about chameleons. See how this one's changed his color to the color of your skin? The light and the change in temperature make him do this. Some people think chameleons change their colors to camouflage themselves but that's not true. They've got a little mechanism in them under the control of their autonomic nervous system and when they get nervous or excited or anything like that then the pigment in their melanophore cells—"

"Calvin," said Annie.

"What?"

"I am not afraid this chameleon will bite me. When I was a little kid I used to play with them. My father taught me all about them. How about just shutting up?"

Calvin raised his arm to his nose and nuzzled it. The two under the oak trees looked out into the street. It was midmorning—long past time for the neighborhood fortissimo to have begun but there was nothing in the street except the steadily strengthening sunlight.

Calvin went to the table for another cup of water. "Bryant Cape wrote a play," he said. "My mother and I went to see it. He fainted right in the middle of it and they had to carry him out. Somebody poured water on him and his cummerbund faded all red on his shirt and he screamed. He thought somebody had stabbed him."

There was a little wrenching pain in Annie's neck. Against her will it drew her head around so that she faced the dictionary. Within the cord of her glazed vision the big book appeared as a relentless enemy. Now that it had gotten a good hold on her it was never going to let her go. She was fast becoming married to it the way people become married to each other. With her looks and other shortcomings it would probably be the only marriage partner she would ever have. She hated it.

"A cummerbund," softly informed Calvin, "is a sash men wear when they get all dressed up. Women wear them too sometimes. Bryant Cape's was red. It faded all over his shirt. He thought it was blood. He thought one of his relatives had stabbed him because that's what his play was about. He said it was easy to write. All he did was write about his aunt and uncle and cousins. I was wondering why you didn't do that. I think writing a play about your relatives would be a lot easier than writing a book."

"I don't have any relatives," said Annie. "Except you and your mother and my father."

Slowly and carefully Calvin said, "No, there are two more. They live in the woods somewhere not far from here. My mother told me about them. Their name isn't Jelks. It's something else. They live in the woods."

Annie pulled her ear lobes and rubbed her nervous bumps. "I don't know who you're talking about, Calvin. I wish you'd hush. I'm trying to think."

"Stockton," said Calvin. "That's their name. Aunt Callie and Uncle Martin Stockton. That's their name. They do funny things my mother said. You could write a play about them. About the time you and my mother and grandfather went to visit them and my mother was pregnant with me and everybody went off fishing except her and she locked herself in Aunt Callie's laundry room and tried to crawl out through the transom and got stuck because her stomach was so big and a stranger came to use the telephone and he saw my mother hanging up there in the door and he thought—"

"Calvin."

"What?"

"Shut up. The Stocktons aren't any real relation to us. They're just my father's friends. I don't want to write a play about them. I don't want to write a play about anybody. I want to write a book. I'm going to make myself famous with it."

Calvin was taking a pencil from the caddy on the table. He examined its point and eraser. He picked two sheets of paper from the yellow pile and trotted to his rocker. He grinned at her. "While you're writing your book I'm going to write a play."

The idea in the back of Annie's mind was looming larger, taking on direction and design. Her book would be about a good, homely girl, twelve years old, whose reputation had been torn to shreds by malicious tale bearers. There had been a scandal of some sort in the girl's family and the story of it had fallen into the hands of some pretty uncharitable people who were not entrepreneurial. They were all lazy old mules, unable to think or talk about anything except other people. They were so pedantic that they thought this calumny was evidence of their own virtuosity but it wasn't because every one of these gossips sitting around in their unkempt houses, prattling about the good, homely girl's misfortune, (her name would be Catherine Rosalind Kingston) developed a cruel, rare disease which crippled their tongues. Their tongues turned to stone in their mouths; they ossified. Doctors were flown in from all over the world to look at the tongues and they sliced off little pieces of them and studied them under their microscopes but the problem was an enigma to them and they finally had to admit it. They all went home. Catherine Rosalind Kingston could have told them the cause and remedied the situation but she didn't. Not for a whole year. For a year she let the old mules and baboons suffer. At the end of the year Catherine Rosalind Kingston relented and called all the prattlers together and told them the cause of their ossified tongues —gossip. They didn't believe her though, in the way lots of people don't believe the truth. So they went to their graves with their tongues turned to stone inside their mouths. So the town was peaceful and nice after that the way it had been before all the gossip. Catherine and her father, who were both famous druggists, were invited to join the church. They sang in the choir every Sunday.

In her open-air office under the oak trees Annie typed her story and Calvin wrote his play in longhand. They drank six pitchers of ice water, ate a platter of fried chicken and a whole butterscotch pie. They watched two catbirds and a snake have a fight in the westernmost corner of the yard. The snake was merely trying to sun himself on a lower branch of the bay tree there. He tried to slither away from the birds but they wouldn't let him alone. They screamed at him and swooped and darted and pecked. The snake attempted to fight back but the birds were too much for him. They pecked holes in him and presently he fell to the ground, streaming with blood.

"He'll die in a minute," predicted Annie. "And then I suppose I'll have to dig a hole and bury him. Ruth's scared to death of even dead snakes. I just hate anything like that. That snake wasn't hurting those birds. I oughta go get my slingshot and kill them."

It was one o'clock in the afternoon but still, strangely, the neighborhood remained quiet. It was very hot—the thermometer on the front porch registered ninety-eight degrees. Seeking coolness, the goldfish in their pond had hidden themselves between rocks and under lily pads, and the zinnias and marigolds, which should have been standing upright in their beds, dropped their heat-exhausted heads. Even the silent houses along the street seemed to sag in the heat.

"Ruth said everybody's gone swimming," reported Calvin. "They've gone to a lake camp. A big bus came for all of them even before we got out of bed. They took watermelon and fried chicken and all kinds of good stuff to eat. I wonder why we weren't invited."

Annie said, "Well, Calvin, you'd better learn right now that we aren't very popular in this town because people are jealous of us. You see this nice house we live in and the way Ruth keeps it. You see the man come once a week to keep our yard pretty. You see what a nice family we are. My father's smarter than any man in this town. He saves lives every day but you never hear him bragging about it the way Judge Jackson does when he sends some poor old criminal up to prison in Raiford. He did that one time to one of Ruth's friends. One of Ruth's friends stole a car that wasn't even worth twenty-five dollars; he needed it to get to his job every day. But Judge Jackson sent him to Raiford for a whole year. Isn't that awful?"

"Awful," whispered Calvin. "But Ruth's friend shouldn't have stolen that car."

"And that terrible Gwendolyn Ross's father down at the bank. He doesn't own it, he just works there. He's the loan officer. But he never loans anybody any money, not unless they don't need it. If they're rich he says yes when people ask him for a loan but if they're poor he says no. So then the poor people—if they're sick and need drugs—go to my father and he helps them. He never tells anybody though. The only reason I know about it is because I've seen it happen."

Calvin had leaned forward to stare at her. His smile was eager and lovely.

"The people in this town are just green jealous of us because we're more respectable than they are," continued Annie. "We're good Christians and don't need to go to church to prove it. We pay our bills and mind our own business and we never gossip and our characters . . . our characters are good."

"Yes," agreed Calvin. "Yes."

"So that answers your question. We're better than most people in this town and they know it. Hateful, gossipmongering old mules. I would rather be a turnip than be like them. Of course I'm never going to be. You see this book I've started? It's going to make the name of Jelks famous. It's going to make me rich."

Calvin was fanning himself with his bush hat. His little professor face patiently bore the heat of the breathless afternoon. "Yes," he agreed. "I think you'll be rich and famous someday. Ruth and Grandfather always say how smart you are and I believe them."

Annie's voice coming from her throat so unexpectedly high, so thrilled with pleasure, startled her. "Ruth and my father tell you that? They say how smart I am? Really? Really, Calvin?"

"Yes. They tell me that almost every day in private. Both of them. It's so hot. I wish we could go swimming. I wish it would rain. I wish we could go to Grandfather's drugstore where it's cooler."

In that hour Annie almost loved Calvin. With a feeling of generosity new to her she consented to take him to the drugstore and overrode the protests of Jimmy Sass, who didn't like anybody else messing around behind his soda fountain when he was on duty, to let Calvin make his own ice-cream soda, an enormous beige-colored confection topped with a tassle of whipped cream and four maraschino cherries. While Calvin, standing on a box, mixed and dipped and squirted, Jimmy stood at one end of the fountain with his arms tightly folded. He made Annie think of an oak cask; he was shaped like one. His face appeared to have been unplanned, his round little nose slightly off center, pale, fluid eyes too far apart, stiff toothbrush eyebrows, one elevated higher than the other. Jimmy was sixteen and liked girls younger than himself but not Annie. He kept a high, clear polish on his nails, maintained his gravy-colored curls with hair spray, and was in love with himself. To Annie this last was a wicked trait. She could hardly stand Jimmy.

Together Jimmy and Annie stood at the end of the soda fountain watching Calvin concoct his big ice-cream drink. "You shouldn't bring him down here," said Jimmy.

Annie thrust her jaw. "Why not? His grandfather owns this store."

For a long moment Jimmy sought his lame reason. Finally he said it, "You just shouldn't, that's all. You know how people are. Also it's against the health laws to have him back of the fountain. Make him hurry up and get out."

Annie said nothing to Calvin. She waved to her father working in his glass cage. She let her eyes wander around the neat, air-conditioned store. There was a little drop of pain in her stomach. Even this creep, she thought. If it wasn't for my father he wouldn't have two extra dimes to rub together. He'd be out stealing the money his mother won't give him. He steals from my father and my father forgives him. I remember the two times he's been caught. Dumb baboon. Conceited slob.

Jimmy had stopped watching Calvin. He had taken a short emery board from his pocket and was filing his nails. "Your friends went by just a minute ago. Suedella Jackson and Willis Weeks. They'll be back before long. They come in every afternoon about this time. I think Suedella's beautiful. Don't you?"

Annie said, "If all that makeup she wears on her face ever fell off it'd crack the sidewalk."

The emery board in Jimmy's clean, white fingers flashed back and forth across the tips of his nails. "I don't understand why she goes around with that Willis Weeks. You know Willis. What d'you suppose she sees in him?"

Something pecked at Annie's heart. She looked at Jimmy and a high notion began to idly skip around in the back of her mind. She watched Calvin who was climbing down from his box, carefully holding his drink aloft. She said, "Jimmy, your question absolutely amazes me. You're so sophisticated and worldly; everybody says so. Yet you haven't been able to figure out why Suedella goes around with Willis Weeks?"

Jimmy Sass looked sophisticated and worldly. He put a bored look on his face. He took a step to glance at his image in the back-bar mirror. "I never really tried to figure it out. I don't know why I mentioned it just now. It's just that every afternoon they come in here together and . . . well, I was just wonderin' what Willis has that other guys haven't got."

Annie was watching Calvin carry his big glass to one of the little marble-topped tables. "Suedella Jackson," she said, "is starved for love. She told me that one time. But she can't find anybody to satisfy her hunger. Willis doesn't but she can't find anybody else. Suedella's a little nearsighted. There are a lot of boys in this town more forceful than Willis but . . . well, you know, it isn't a girl's place to make the first move. And Suedella's so beautiful she scares men off."

"More forceful," said Jimmy. "What d'you mean by that?"

"Suedella told me one time that she'd just like to have some man rush up to her and grab her and chew her ear off," came Annie's slow response. "She's very passionate. It doesn't show but she is."

"It shows," croaked Jimmy. "Boy, does it show! *I'd* like to chew her ear off! But she's always with Willis and I just can't go running up to her and . . . not in here. Not with Willis and everybody watching. She doesn't scare *me* off but . . . well, I don't know. I've just been watching her."

"Jimmy," said Annie. "I can't help you with *all* your problems. I was just trying to help you with *one*. Of course you can't go running up to her when Willis is around. You should pick a time when he isn't. Don't you make deliveries to the Jacksons all the time? Sometimes don't you deliver things to Suedella's house at night?"

"Yeah," answered Jimmy. "I make deliveries sometimes to Suedella's house at night. And Willis isn't always there. I just never thought . . . well, isn't it funny how you don't think about things sometimes until other people mention them?"

"Funny," murmured Annie and went to the back of the store and had a little peaceful visit with her father:

"You're too skinny," remarked Doc Jelks.

"Look who's talking," retorted Annie.

They laughed together. It was like old times before she had got to be so big and twelve years old. Her father asked what she and Calvin had been doing and she told him about her book and Calvin's play. She noticed the tiredness in his face and asked when he was going to close the store and take his annual vacation.

"In a week or two," he told her.

"Are we going someplace or are we just going to stay home and rest?"

Her father was humming one of his ballads but broke off to answer her. "We're going to get in the car and go visit the Stocktons for a few days. You remember them. Your Aunt Callie and Uncle Martin."

Suedella and Willis had come in. They were sitting at the fountain and Jimmy was serving them. Calvin was sucking at the last of his drink. The phone in the prescription booth rang and her father answered it; he had a friendly conversation with one of his customers.

It was very peaceful.

A day or two after that Suedella Jackson and Gwendolyn Ross came to the Jelkses' front gate. They stood outside it, rattling its latch and imperiously calling to Annie and after a minute she left her books and Calvin and went out as far as the steps. She sat down on the topmost one and regarded her two former friends. Gwendolyn had her arm around Suedella and appeared to be supporting her. The murky twilight wavered uncertainly around them. A little white bandage shone on one of Suedella's ears.

Annie rested her elbows on her knees; she leaned forward and wrinkled her forehead. "Hey," she said. "What're you-all doing?"

Suedella raised her clenched fists and shook them at Annie. "You terrible girl!" she screamed. "I ought to have you arrested! I ought to have my father put you in jail!"

Annie drew back, staring. "Are you talking to me, Suedella? If you are I don't understand you. Why on earth should you want to have me arrested? What have I done?"

"You told Jimmy Sass . . . that vile, that *awful* boy that I was passionate!" shrieked Suedella. "And that I was starved for love and wanted some man just to rush up to me and chew my ear off!"

Annie fingered her hair and rubbed the soles of her

tough feet together. "Suedella, you can't have me arrested for saying that. You told me that and you know you did. You can't have me arrested for just repeating the truth. Can you?"

"Ohhhhhhhh," moaned Suedella. "I just hate you! You and that terrible Jimmy Sass!"

"Did he attack you, Suedella? If he did you can have him arrested. Was there a witness? Did you tell your father?"

"He didn't attack me!" bawled Suedella. "And don't go around telling people he did! I'd just die if . . . we were just sitting in my living room . . . I just asked him to sit down for a minute and he did . . . but then he started talking about how passionate you said I was and he grabbed me by the ear and started chewing on it! Like it was something to *eat!* Oh, I've never been so humiliated! You told him to do it! You put him up to it and don't you dare deny it, Annie Jelks!"

"How disgusting," said Annie. "I think ears are the ugliest parts of the human body. I know mine are." She rose and went back into the house. Now it had grown too dark to read without the aid of artificial light. She switched on a lamp and took up her book. She couldn't concentrate on the words; her fingers trembled when she turned the pages. In his room Calvin was playing with his anatomy man. She could hear him shuffling back and forth between the man and the box of plastic organs. She hated him.

CHAPTER SEVEN

THE MERCHANDISE AT the library occupied her days. She lugged great stacks of books home and savagely devoured them. She didn't love them the way Calvin and Miss Dishman did; they didn't reassure her. They drenched her in despair. They were perfect and she herself would never be able to write one. Some had their shortcomings but in spite of this they were all so perfectly assembled, so perfectly managed.

The dream of her own possibilities as a storyteller turned grim and sore. Angry and frustrated she mulled over the pages of her own production—the story about the people with the ossified tongues. It wasn't possible, it wasn't real. Besides that her choice of words was too grandiose. How in the name of thunder did you learn how to select words? Which to pick and which to reject?

It was August, the month of the recital. She applied herself to the business of mastering the piece she would play. Fortissimo. Pianissimo. Fortissimo. Crescendo! Ah, curses on the luck and curses on the cretin who had invented the piano.

She was required to go to town with Ruth to buy her recital dress. They were to look for something "nice and pretty." After an hour of pawing through the dress racks Ruth said she could take her pick between a tan suit and a light blue sailor outfit. The suit brought out the sallow tones in her skin and the sailor outfit accentuated the apple sized paunch beneath her ribs. Standing before the full-length mirror in the dress shop she bitterly estimated her image. "Twelve years old and already I look like an old scrubwoman. I've got a paunch on me and this dress doesn't do anything to hide it."

"I wish my paunch wasn't any bigger than yours," said Ruth. "Come on now. We haven't got all day. Which is it going to be? The blue or the tan?"

"They're sacks," said Annie. "They're both perfectly itless colors. Why do I have to wear such itless colors? Why can't I have something with sequins on it? Or lace? Pink maybe. Or red."

They went home with the tan suit and a pair of new white shoes. The shoes made her feet look like boats. To distract from them she conceived the idea of sneaking back to town to buy an orange feather boa. The round, fluffed scarf draped around her shoulders heightened her color and gave personality to the suit. She sprayed it with Lanvin's My Sin perfume, gleaned from the sample bar in her father's store, and hid it in her closet.

She went now every afternoon to Professor Evans' music studio. To simulate recital night conditions the piano was draped with a silver shawl which kept sliding off, adding to the other distractions—Professor Evans' heavy breathing, the metronome clacking, the sweat prickling at her scalp and between her shoulder blades. Professor Evans loomed over her, exhaling noisily. He wore a green tie with domino-shaped characters in it. He strode up and down, silently counting with the metronome, and his long, limp hair hung down across his forehead. He carried a ruler and when she struck wrong notes the ruler would come down to stay her hands. He would peer at her, his brilliant eyes bewildered and imploring. "Why do you fight with the piano? It is not your enemy. Play the music as it is written, this part soft, this part loud. Pianissimo. Fortissimo. You've switched them around and it isn't right. And all those little half notes in this passage here. Where are you getting them from?"

"From my head," replied Annie. "Right along in here it needs something to dress it up a little. The audience will get bored if I don't do that. The guy who wrote this might have been a great composer but seems like to me he forgot what he was doing along about here. Seems to me like he kind of lost his nerve. Isn't this whole thing supposed to be a diatribe? That's my interpretation of it. It's a diatribe against something or another he was mad at but right along about in here he lost his nerve."

Professor Evans' long, creamy nose quivered. "A diatribe? Where did you get that word? Who told you that?"

"Nobody. I just thought it. Well, all right, maybe it isn't a diatribe. But he was mad when he wrote it and it sounds good, after you get used to it, up until the time when you get to this part. Then it gets kind of foppish."

"It's a little half-waltz," declared Professor Evans. "Its simplicity is lovely. You must play it as it is written. Again please. Try it again." He stood in back of her with the ruler in his hand poised. His clothes emitted the odor of starch. His breath, coming and going from him, was audible. The silver shawl on the piano slid sideways, hesitated and slipped to the floor. Annie rose from her bench and retrieved it. She started to return it to the piano top but Professor Evans said, "Never mind, never mind. Here, give it to me. Play. Just for heaven's sake sit down and play."

She sat down and played her whole recital piece from beginning to end. Pianissimo so soft, fortissimo so loud, with all of her strength behind it. The notes came whanging from the piano and for the first time they were exact and correct.

"Good," wheezed Professor Evans. "That's very good. But try to remember not to slump over the keyboard. Sit erect. The pianist on stage should always be a little bit of an exhibitionist. Don't droop your hands like that. Keep them raised like this. You see? Your hands are really quite nice. There isn't a thing wrong with trying to show them off a little when you play."

Annie darted a look at her hands. Professor Evans was lying. Her hands were like her ears and feet—too big. They were too brown from the sun and the nails were ragged. Before the recital she would go to a beauty shop and have a professional manicure. She would have that and wear the orange boa and she would play as she had never played before and everybody would see that she wasn't a bit like Norma who would have worn the tan suit with nothing colorful to dress it up and coolly played each note as it was written. She wasn't Norma. She was herself and she would show everybody she was. There would be plaudits and she would receive these courteously. Her father would be proud of her.

Swinging her music case by its handle Annie trudged home. Going through the vacant lots she observed a flock of birds rising from the ground in a swift, impressive pattern. When they were in the sky they fanned out and flew into the soundless wind and presently were lost in the atmosphere. Watching them, she stood very still. It was the first time she had ever really looked at birds in flight. All those birds just shooting up into the air like that, so free. It was very queer. That night when her father came home she spoke to him of it: "They came straight up out of the ground, out of some weeds. And they went straight up; I never saw anything go so fast. And then they disappeared."

With an interested expression her father looked at her. "When I was a kid I was always looking at birds. I was especially interested in the cause of migration and I remember I became very involved in this. Did you know that migrating birds often travel several hundred miles in a single day or a single night?"

Annie clasped her hands around her knees and looked out into the yard. In the corners there were lairs of darkness. The wind riffled through the patch of grass between the sidewalk outside their gate and the curb and there were frail night sounds. She hadn't meant to bring up anything so ponderous as the migration of birds. She had meant only to say how it had felt to witness the birds that afternoon—how free and light it had made her feel.

"If I had not decided to be a pharmacist I might easily have become an ornithologist," said Doc Jelks.

It was another word to be looked up. She didn't even know how to spell it and the dictionary was inside the house and she didn't want to leave her peaceful post on the porch. Without thinking, Annie said, "Aw, rats and piffle," and her father laughed and the phone inside the house rang and it was Norma, calling from California.

Alone on the porch Annie sat in the cooling darkness and half listened to her father's end of the phone conversation floating out through the open door. Her father was proud of Norma in a way that he would never be proud of her, Annie. Norma had a thing called integrity and she had a rare kind of courage. She was generous— she had given their father Calvin to adore and he truly did this. Each night before he went to his own bed her father looked in on Calvin; he would rearrange the sheets and feel Calvin's skin and kiss him. The love her father felt for Calvin was an almost embarrassing thing to watch. It made Annie's stomach squinch just to think of it.

She rose and went down into the yard and walked around and around waiting for the telephone conversation with Norma to end. But her father's voice, with little speckles of pleasure in it, went on and on. And the light, free feeling in her went away.

It was recital night and Ruth was rushing around managing things. Calvin loitered in his bath and she yelled at him to hurry. She discovered a berry juice stain on the lapel of Doc Jelks' white linen suit and this had to be removed before he could put it on. She slammed supper on the table and commanded everybody to eat and be quick about it. Stolidly calm, Annie forced down a great helping of creamed chipped beef on biscuit and a serving of banana pudding.

"I'm a little nervous," said her father. "Are you?"

She grinned at him. "No. It's nothing. Just a little old recital."

"We're going to sit in the front row and watch you," declared Calvin. "And you had better play better than Shack Vareen, you better had."

The jacket to her tan suit hid her paunch. She brushed her hair back in little duck tufts and her professional manicure glittered and she was very calm. She gathered her music case, her purse, and the bag containing the boa and went to stand on the porch beside Ruth and Calvin. Her father was backing the car out, bringing it around to the curb.

"What's in the bag?" asked Ruth.

"Shoes," answered Annie. "For afterward. In case my father decides to take us someplace for a little celebration. These I've got on hurt a little so I've got this extra pair along." She was going to make this night a cause for a Jelks celebration. The lie was excusable—Ruth would forgive her for it afterward.

The Women's Club was lighted. There were baskets of flowers at the door and more on the stage. Some of the society women of the town were acting as ushers. Dressed in their bright summer dresses they were herding people into the auditorium and seating them. Some of the old people from The Gray Moss Inn were occupying half a row. They sat placidly with their wrinkled hands folded and their gray faces solemnly awaited the entertainment. Doc Jelks, Calvin, and Ruth were given seats in the sixth row. Ruth said the air-conditioning was pleasant. She fussed with Calvin's socks and avoided the looks from the Jacksons and the Rosses who were seated just across the aisle. Doc lifted his hand to Judge Jackson and the judge nodded.

Suedella and Mrs. Jackson looked at and through the Jelkses and Ruth. Suedella had on blue gloves to match her dress and her little garden variety face was perfect, as if someone had painted it and then attached it to her body.

Carrying her music case, her purse, and the bag containing the feather boa, Annie left the auditorium and went to the room back of the stage where the rest of the participants in the recital were already gathered. They sat on chairs and fussed with their clothes and their hair. They whispered to each other and made silly conversation. They were all younger than Annie except Shack Vareen who sat stiffly away from the others.

Annie set her things on the floor in a corner and walked up and down, pumping her arms and legs, trying to rid herself of the knot of indigestion that had formed in her stomach.

After a minute of coldly watching this, Shack said, "Oh, do sit down. You're making me so nervous."

Annie sat on a chair next to Shack. She lolled her feet and fingered her hair. "But it's nothing," she said. "Just a little old recital. You shouldn't be nervous, Shack. Everybody in town says you play like an angel. You look like one, too. I wish I had hair like yours. Now if you played like me and looked like me you'd have something to worry about. Say, I wonder where Professor Evans is. Oh, here he comes. Oh, my, look at him. He's gorgeous. I didn't know he could look like that, did you? What's that thing in his eye?"

"It's a monocle," answered Shack and turned sideways in her chair. "Please don't talk. Just please be quiet. Can't you see how nervous I am?" The substance beneath her skin looked as if it was melting. She was the first to go on and as she left the room to walk out on the stage her legs wobbled. Annie felt sorry for her. In just a minute or two she was back, white-faced and crying. Professor Evans was with her and he was very upset. He put Shack in a chair and sent a little kid out for water.

"How much water?" asked the little kid. "And what should I bring it in?" And Professor Evans ran out for it himself, almost colliding with Shack's mother who was just coming in to the room, and the people in the auditorium were making restless sounds and Professor

Evans came running back with a coffee can filled with water and a paper cup and thrust these at Shack's mother and then he sprinted over to Annie and hissed that she should go on next.

"It's not my turn," she said. "I'm supposed to be the third one to go on but if you think it'll calm the people down out there, I'll do it. Wait just a second—I need to get something out of . . . hey, who stole my boa? Oh, here it is; nobody stole it. They just shoved it back underneath this chair. There now. How do I look, Professor? You think I'll wow 'em?"

The boa wasn't making any kind of impression on Professor Evans because the little kid who had been sent for the water but didn't go was threatening to leave and go home and a couple of the other little kids were showing apprehension—they were sniffling and looking at Shack who now lay on two chairs and was violently trembling—and Professor Evans was on his knees trying to gather them around and comfort them.

She wasn't sure whether she should be announced. When Shack went on she hadn't been paying attention. But after a moment of indecision she walked out on the stage by herself. She walked across it to the piano and stood beside it and looked down across the footlights to the sea of faceless faces. She grinned at the dim audience and felt some of the figures in it jerk to attention. The cross currents from the cool, air-conditioned air lifted the boa from the back of her neck and the feathers curled softly around her ears. The boat shoes were painfully squeezing her feet but she lightly hopped around the piano bench and seated herself at the glistening keyboard. Someone had taped the silver shawl to the piano top so that it wouldn't slide. The perfume from her boa lifted to her nostrils in a heady wave. This was the night of Annie Jelks. She raised her hands and placed them on the keyboard and struck the first chord.

The little half-waltz in the center of her piece brought a curious response from the audience. She leaned to it and romped through it and someone beyond the footlights groaned and a voice like Calvin's cried, "It's Annie! Listen to her go!"

She lifted her head and a tip of the boa blew into her face. Through the orange feathers she saw her enemies, the Jacksons and the Rosses and the old baboons from The Gray Moss Inn. Vague figures in the darkened auditorium, they were leaning forward watching and listening and it was high triumph. She was showing them who she was.

But nobody except her own family came up to her afterward. The society women ushered the people from the auditorium and they stood in knots on the sidewalks laughing and talking and presently got into their cars and drove away.

Doc Jelks drove his family to The Dinner Bell for a little celebration. They ate hamburgers and drank iced tea and Doc Jelks couldn't say it often enough—how much he had enjoyed the recital, especially Annie's part in it.

"Well," she said, "at least I didn't almost pass out like Shack Vareen. Did you see Professor Evans' monocle?

And that suit he had on? What kind of suit was that he had on anyway?"

"An evening suit," replied her father. "A tuxedo. Pretty grand for this little burg."

"It was nice," sighed Annie. "But I don't know. I don't think I want to be a pianist. I didn't invent the piano and I can't write music and . . . I don't know. It isn't something you do all by yourself."

Doc Jelks sent Ruth home in a cab and they went home in their car. Calvin went straight to bed and Annie went to her room and eased her feet from the boat shoes and stored the orange boa on a shelf in her closet. She would never wear it again.

She sat in the middle of her bed and studied the pages of her story concerning the people with the ossified tongues. Now the big, grand words in it seemed forced and already she had forgotten the meanings of half of them.

Anyway what good is it, she asked herself. Nobody knows I'm writing it except Ruth and my father and Calvin and Miss Dishman. Even if I did write it good enough to make me famous nobody would care.

On this day Annie abandoned the library and books.

CHAPTER EIGHT

THE INDOLENCE OF the summer days nettled her. She stretched a hammock between two trees in the front yard and lay in it with her bare, dirty feet pointing up yearning for something to happen. For a hurricane to come rolling in out of the Gulf of Mexico and slam into them, for a meteor to tailspin across the sky and drop into the town erasing it all except Jelks' Drugstore and the Jelkses' home. For a snow-covered mountain to suddenly appear in the center of the street. Even for school to start. Anything with action in it. At least with the opening of the school term she would be able to look forward to some good fights. Maybe just to be prepared she should send for a book on judo or karate.

Dressed in her old gym shorts and a sleeveless shirt which had grown too small, Annie lay on her back in her hammock, solemnly eyeing her paunch through slitted eyes, deliciously contemplating a vision of herself as victor in a judo contest with Suedella Jackson or Gwendolyn Ross or Willis Weeks. In this dream Suedella was her favorite opponent. Suedella would start the fight of course and Annie would take a lot of her nastiness before she'd finally turn and defend herself. Then she'd rush up to Suedella and with all of the skill of the game at her command throw Suedella to the ground and place a foot on her stomach. While Suedella was going down she'd sock her a couple of times in the old kisser. Suedella would cough out a couple of teeth and her nose would pour blood and the consequences that Ruth and her father would mete out would be worth every second of it. Thinking about it, Annie laughed out loud and Calvin, who had just come from the house, walked over to the hammock and peered at her. "What's funny?" he asked.

"Nothing, Calvin. Go read or something. Go away."

Calvin sat down on the grass. "Grandfather just came home. He's in the house right now talking to Ruth. Tomorrow we're going to Uncle Martin Stockton's for a visit. Ruth's not going; she's going to take a separate vacation."

Annie sat up. "Calvin, why is it you always know everything before I do?"

Beneath his hat, Calvin's head wagged. "I don't know. It just happens. Uncle Martin's got lots of cows and Grandfather's going to teach me about them. He's going to teach us both how to fish. We're going to see raccoons and wild pigs and lots of things. Grandfather wants you to come in and see about the things you want to take. Ruth's going to pack us a big lunch; she doesn't want us to stop in any old greasy-spoon restaurant."

Annie rose and swaggered toward the house. At the steps she turned and looked back at Calvin. "We're going to stay two weeks!" he shouted and threw his bush hat into the air.

Directed by her father they went in a free and easy style. "People plan too much for vacations," said Doc Jelks. "By the time they get through with all their planning and packing they're worn out. The only way to go is like this. Just throw your clothes into the car like this, see? And then your fishing gear. And then your lunch to eat along the way. And then you hop in yourself and take off. See how easy it is? No worrying and no fussing. No haranguing and harassing and wearing yourself out. Just everything nice and free and easy." Doc Jelks lifted his fine, tenor voice in song and they rolled out of the driveway and the sunlight, already hot and strong, splashed across the hood of the car—a good omen.

Alone in the back seat of the car Annie lolled her feet and patted her ears. To be away from it all—the people who knew about Calvin. To be away from the dictionary and the feeling that she must do something before the summer ended to prove herself—ah, it was good. Pleased with these conditions, Annie slumped into a corner of the seat and listened to her father sing and soon they were out of the hated town, taking a back road that wound around pristine lakes and through deep scrub country. They went across the great southern plain and saw a deer bounding away through the underbrush and wild turkey gobblers, chestnut feathers shining in the sun, racing through the trees.

They ate a ten-o'clock lunch beside a sinkhole, a great,

ancient depression in white limestone, caused by subterranean water passages. Springs bubbled at the bottom of this, running away from the shallow pool they formed to become lost in the beginning of an underground stream. They went down into the hole and found that the water was icy cold. Calvin dropped his glasses and a school of minnows darted to them but then swam away disappearing into a windrow of bubbles. Above the hole and just a few feet away from it the hammock was warm and dusky green, and the gray moss hanging in the trees was gently stirred with each puff of wind.

They came to the Stocktons' place, sprawled across forty acres, before noon. There was the low, white house remembered from Annie's earlier childhood, the white barns and the scuppernong arbors. On a rise of land above the farmhouse they saw brown cattle grazing and beyond them there was a figure on a horse riding along a stretch of undulating field fence. Erect on his horse he seemed to be looking for something.

"That's Martin," said Doc Jelks and they stood in the driveway beside the car for a moment and watched and presently they saw the object of this—a lone cow, mammoth in size, stealthily emerging from a stand of live oaks. When it saw the rider it stopped and pawed the earth and even across the distance this seemed to be a menacing thing.

Callie Stockton had come from the house to pump their hands and bawl, "Welcome!" and they asked her about the scene taking place on the rise. "Aw, that's not a cow!" she shouted. "That's a bull! That's Geronimo

and he's crazier'n a bedbug. He's not worth the powder
it would take to blow his brains out. The cows are all
scared to death of him and so am I and so is Martin a
little bit but he won't admit it. He's a fool about that ol'
worthless bull. But come in, come in! Y'all haven't had
your dinner, have you? You have? Aw now, what'd you
want to go and do that for? I got chicken pilau and
mustard greens fresh outa my garden, and mango ice
cream. I churned it myself. What'd you go and eat for?
You should've knowed I'd have plenty cooked and
waitin' fer you. Aw, well, it don't matter. It'll keep."
Callie took a gun from the sideboard in the old-fashioned dining room and went outside and fired two shots
into the air signaling her husband to come home.

The Stocktons had their noon dinner and the Jelkses
ate their share of the mango ice cream which tasted like
strawberry, pineapple, and peach because it had been
made from Haden mangoes, a strange, multiflavored
fruit extravagantly imported from Key West, and during this Annie decided that the Stocktons were two rare
people. They were older than her father but had never
seen snow or been to Cincinnati or even up to Talla-
hassee. They went to town once a month for supplies
and even this trip was regrettable.

"It jest don't hold no attraction fer us," said Martin.
"No town don't offer us ary a thing we ain't got more
of and better of right here. Callie and me's got everything we need right here without one of us gets bad off
sick but that ain't happened yet and it ain't likely to. We

eat good and stay healthy. We're both healthier'n mules."

"Except one time last winter I takened the nosebleed pretty bad," amended Callie. "Martin thought he was going to have to carry me to a doctor but after a while we got it stopped by ourselves. Martin went down to the barns and brought me back a sack full of cobwebs. I packed my nose with 'em and directly the bleeding stopped."

"Cobwebs," said Doc Jelks and carefully scraped his ice-cream plate. "A doctor would have used gauze. He'd have cauterized the bleeding point with a silver nitrate solution. If it happens again try ice on the back of your neck and on the bridge of your nose."

The Stocktons rested their tolerant eyes on Doc Jelks. Across Annie's head and Calvin's they began to talk of other, lighter things—of the way the Jelkses would be entertained during their stay. There were bream and bass in the big lake down on the lower end of the Stocktons' land spread just aching to be caught and there were frogs with edible legs the size of chicken drumsticks (frogging was only done at night) and there were horses to be ridden and lots of other attractions.

"We don't know how to ride horses," said Annie, and Callie turned a grave look on Doc Jelks and said, "Why, Doc, this child don't know you. Let's show her how you can ride a horse."

Astride his great golden beast her father did not look like a pharmacist; he didn't look a bit scholarly or professional. His hat was at a rakish slant and he sat in his saddle easily slouched, enjoying himself, and it occurred to Annie with a little shock that in another time her father had known the kind of life that was here. He hadn't always been a druggist and a father and a grand-father. In another time he had been young and had had good times with people like the Stocktons and had learned how to sit on a horse like that.

Her father was grinning down at her and Calvin. He made a little movement with his feet and hands and the horse lifted his head, did a graceful turn, and galloped away. Annie watched him ride toward the rise in the land where earlier they had seen the crazy bull and she wanted to call to him to be careful, to come back, but the Stocktons were bringing up two other horses, one for her and one for Calvin, and they were explaining how to sit and how the reins should be held and how the rider's legs controlled the horse's haunches and saying not to be afraid.

Calvin might have been born on a horse so easily did he take to his mount. He listened studiously to all the Stocktons' directions. He stroked the animal's head and whispered to it and the animal responded with a gentle flick of his silver mane and a blissful sigh. Calvin pressed his little heels into the horse's sides and said, "Go, horsie," and the horse moved away from the porch steps in a slow, smooth trot.

Annie's horse had the most enormous head she had ever seen on any animal. In her eyes it appeared to be at least six feet long and his round, smooth rump was immense and the place where she was supposed to sit didn't seem a safe place at all. It seemed a preposterous distance to the ground and the horse had turned his head at her and she was positive she saw sly contempt mirrored in his great, dewy eyes. She looked out across the fields and saw her father galloping across the distant rise and saw Calvin trotting around a haystack, his bare head glinting butter-yellow in the sun.

The Stocktons were watching her. Callie was saying, "Now they ain't nothing to it, honey. Just remember what we said and you won't have a bit o' trouble. It ain't dangerous; this old nag wouldn't hurt a flea. Go on; ride him."

Calvin had glommed on to all of their instructions in the same way he glommed on to new dictionary words. The second they had reached his ears he had directed them to his brain and there they would remain forever pasted. This was the big, infuriating difference in them, in her and Calvin. He soaked up learning as easily as he breathed while she had to work and strain for every morsel of it.

Her mind was totally, horribly blank. She couldn't remember how Callie and Martin had said to get the horse going or stopped or turned around or anything. She only knew that Callie and Martin had got her up on the horse and that now it was expected, for some fool reason, for her to ride him. Callie and Martin had gone up on the porch and were brightly watching her. Imitating Calvin she patted the horse's head and whispered to him: "Nice horsie. I won't hurt you. I'll give you a bone when we get back."

The horse stiffened.

"It's got a lot of meat on it," whispered Annie. "I saw it in the refrigerator. I'll snitch it for you. Be nice now. All I want to do is ride you for a few minutes and then we'll come back and I'll give you a bone. Okay? Okay. Well, let's go. Giddap or something. Giddap. *Please* giddap. You're making a fool out of me."

Beneath her the horse's back was tensed rigid. He was leering at her. There was steam coming from his nose and tears stood in his eyes. She patted him again and whispered to him soothingly. "Well, it isn't anything to blubber about. I know I look heavy from the front but actually I'm very skinny. I'm not very heavy. Think about the bone, man. Let's go. Giddap!"

The horse jerked his head around, his back muscles convulsed, he blew steam, he pumped his right front leg, he drew a deep breath and they shot away from the porch in a burst of wild, furious speed. They careened down the driveway and then took out across the fields toward the haystack. She smelled the hay as they tore past the stack and went around it. They went past Calvin and as in a dream she saw his little professor-face agape, the glasses covering his eyes glittering. The field was dry with strange clouds of ocher dust rising up to meet them, to envelop them.

That dust shouldn't rise up in *front* of us, she thought. This fool horse is some kind of a devil. He's got everybody else fooled but not me. *Our father, Who art in Heaven. Hallowed be Thy name. Thy kingdom come. Thy will be done. . . .*

Like something possessed of a demon the horse was roaring around and around the haystack and the steam was pouring from his great, black nostrils and his great, black rump was switching and his great black muscles were rippling and he was making funny, blowing sounds in his throat and she was desperately hanging on. Sometimes the force of the wind against the animal under her would jerk her legs straight out and her head was crazily snapping back and forth so that sight was impossible. "Whooooooeeeeee!" she cried. "Whooooooeeeeee! Stop now! That's enough! All right now . . . you . . . devil . . . you! I . . . won't . . . give . . . you . . . that . . . bone . . . I . . . promised!"

Abruptly the horse came to a braking halt. He backed up to the haystack and reared high. She slid backward over his rump and fell into the hay. The horse trotted off and Calvin came riding over. He peered down at her. "You must've done something wrong," he said. "You must not have been listening when Aunt Callie and Uncle Martin were telling us what to do. See my horse? He does everything I want him to. See? I want him to go forward now so he goes forward. Now I want him to go backward so he goes—"

Tears were not her privilege. She sat up and brushed wisps of hay from her face and hair. "Calvin."

"What, Annie?"

"That horse is a devil. I felt it the minute I got on

him. He hated me. He's some kind of a demon. Did you see the way the dust came up in *front* of us, even before we got to it?"

Calvin looked uncertain.

Annie stood up. Her arms and legs and neck and face were covered with little pricklings of hay and she had to pick each piece off separately because she was covered with sweat, too. "I was going to be good to him, too," she said. "I offered him a big bone with lots of nice meat on it."

Behind his spectacles Calvin squeezed his eyes shut. Then slowly he opened them. His sorrowed gaze was gentle and kind. He lifted his arm to his face and licked the inside of his elbow. In a hushed voice he said, "But, Annie, horses don't eat bones with meat on them. You must've been thinking about a dog when you told him that. Horses eat grass and grain."

Annie picked a long sliver of hay from her hair. She sailed it into the wind. "Well, all right," she said. "But so what? We'll both ride him back to the house. I can't possibly walk that far. Make him kneel down so I can get on."

Calvin's look was incredulous. "Make him kneel down? Oh, I don't think I know how to do that, Annie. This isn't a camel, it's a horse. I don't think horses know how to kneel down to let people get on them."

"If we had a ladder," Annie said and her voice rose on a desperate, foolish note. "But we haven't got one, have we?"

"No," replied Calvin. "I don't have one and I don't see one anywhere around here."

Graceless, sodden with sweat, covered with dust and hay chaff, Annie was obliged to walk back across the fields to the house. She sat on the shady porch and silently suffered. It happened because I'm ignorant, she thought. I'm not even as smart as Callie and Martin, stuffing cobwebs up Callie's nose to stop her nosebleed.

Callie brought her an iced grape drink and Martin said that horsemanship wasn't a thing to be learned in one day. Doc Jelks came back from his ride and Calvin from his and Calvin didn't snitch on her—he didn't say a word about the meaty bone she had promised the horse. Callie brought more iced grape drinks on a tray and Martin settled back and entertained the Jelkses with tales of life in the hammock. Sometimes during spring gobbler season hunters would come to the Stockton place and Martin would go into the piney-woods with them and be their paid guide. In poorer, bygone days the Stocktons had been professional collectors of snakes for a reptile institute. As they had cleared their land they had captured diamondback rattlers, cottonmouth moccasins, and corals, routing them from gopher holes and storing them in canvas bags in their woodshed. Periodically a truck from the institute would come after the snakes and for their deadly prizes the Stocktons would be paid. But that had been a long time ago, before the big, air-cooled house and the scuppernong arbors and the cattle. Now they didn't collect snakes. At their leisure they planted and harvested their crops and raised cattle. Their activities were largely governed by the movements of the moon, the stars, and the sun.

"Out here we pay attention to nature because we're closer to it than you city people are," Martin said. "We feel nature and we live by it and we're healthier for it and happier, too. I swear it'd just kill us off to have to live in town the way you do, Doc. What's its big attraction, can you tell me that?"

Annie's father smiled at his old friend. "I have a family, Martin, and I have to provide for them. I'm not a farmer. But you're right; it's good out here."

"It's the best," declared Martin Stockton. "There's no bigger satisfaction anywhere than to sit out here like this and look out across a spread of land like that out yonder and feel you're as close to what life is all about as any human can get to be. I thank God for it every day of my life. Every evenin' I sit out here like this, watching that old sun barrelling around this old earth and I thank God for putting me here."

Doc Jelks and Callie had risen to walk to the edge of the porch. They were looking toward a distant ridge and Callie was saying, "There's that crazy bull again. Look at him. Sometimes he stands there for hours like that without moving a muscle. And then he'll take a fit o' runnin' and he runs till he drops. I swear he's crazier'n a bedbug. I wish you'd do something about him, Martin. Sell him or something."

Martin's reply was lazy. "I'd get rid of him if he was

hurtin' anything. But he ain't. He's old and harmless. Don't worry about him, Callie. Don't look at him if it pains you."

The adults on the porch returned to their talk. They spoke of the simpler days of the past and the complicated ones of the present. They talked about the affairs of the nation and the high cost of living. Callie said there were some political crooks in Washington and Doc Jelks agreed with her.

The adult talk was inviting a headache. Calvin looked as if he already had one. He was studying Martin Stockton intently and his little sweated face was all squinched up and there were little kinks of hurt in his big green eyes. He tiptoed across the porch to Annie and whispered: "Take me for a walk, Annie. Let's go see the grapes."

They went around the house to the scuppernong arbors and sat on upturned flower pots beneath one. They looked up at the espaliered tangle of vines and wire and Calvin admired the heavily clustered fruit, shining pale, silver-green among the dark leaves.

"You can eat some if you want," she said.

Calvin shook his head. "Not now. Annie, did you hear what Uncle Martin said about the sun?"

"Of course. What about it?"

Calvin's expression was grave and anxious. He squirmed on his flower pot. "He said he watched the sun go around the earth and it doesn't. The earth goes around the sun. You know how I know? I've got a book

on planets. The sun is a star and the earth goes around
it. So why did Uncle Martin say it was the other way
around?"

"I don't know, Calvin, I don't know. I think I've got
a headache. Uncle Martin's a good man. What difference does it make whether he believes the sun goes
around the earth instead of the earth going around the
sun? It doesn't change anything. Curses. I *know* I've got
a headache. Don't talk any more. Eat some grapes."

Calvin was polishing his glasses on the hem of his dirty
shorts. He was looking at her.

Avoiding his gaze, Annie lolled her feet and fingered
her hair. After a minute she said, "All right, so I didn't
know it either. But that's not a crime. A lot of people
don't know a lot of things. I read books all the time and
the more I read the dumber I get. Maybe Uncle Martin's
the same way. Eat some grapes and shut up."

In deepest gloom Calvin continued to look at her and
he didn't reach up for any of the grapes. "Uncle Martin
and Aunt Callie don't have any books," he said. "I
looked. They don't have a one. I asked Aunt Callie and
she said they didn't have any. She said they didn't like
to read."

"Oh," moaned Annie. "Oh, oh. First the horse and
now this."

"And I didn't bring any either," insisted Calvin in
mounting anxiety. "I had a pile all picked out to bring
but then I forgot them. And we're miles and miles from
a library and I can't ask anybody to take me. Can I?"

"Oh," moaned Annie. "I don't know why you're in

my life. I honestly don't. I wish you weren't. I honestly wish you weren't."

Calvin left the flower pot and the scuppernong arbor. Through slitted eyes, because the pain in her head was now an actual one, she watched his browned legs beneath the dirty shorts carry his little professor-body back across the brittle lawn grass and up the back steps of the house. She lowered her head to her hands and bit her knuckles.

CHAPTER NINE

GRANDLY the Stocktons hosted the Jelkses. Callie's meals, even her breakfasts served the minute dawn cracked, were feasts. Doc Jelks and Martin taught Calvin how to lasso posts and roosters and how to catch fish. On occasions where riding a horse was required Annie shared Calvin's mount. The animal would go anywhere Calvin wanted him to go and do anything he wanted him to do except kneel down to let Annie get on. She had to learn the trick of mounting the animal while Calvin and the horse patiently waited.

Back in the wild tangle of the region surrounding the Stocktons' place, Calvin was disappointed in the absence of the promised wild pigs.

"Civilization has moved in and takened 'em all away," lamented Martin. "But never mind; there are other things just as interestin'. You ever eat swamp cabbage?"

Calvin confessed that he never had and Martin, axe in hand, selected a young palm tree and cut it down. Expertly Callie removed its tough outer layers and withdrew a creamy, waxen cylinder. She held it up: "Swamp cabbage. Up north folks pay a lot of money for it. Down here it's free but we don't have it too often because the only way you can get it is to kill the whole tree and we don't like to do that."

The pinders, a whole field of them, were mature enough to be stripped from their vines. "What are pinders?" asked Calvin, and Callie, with a look of genuine surprise said, "Why, young 'un, ain't you ever heard o' pinders? Pinders is peanuts. For gracious sakes, don't they teach you *anything* out in California?"

In the broiling sun Annie, Calvin, and Callie pulled pinders, filling two buckets. They carried them back to the house, washed them in cold water and boiled them for six hours, using plenty of salt. They were juicy and good; much better than walnuts or chestnuts, Calvin declared.

The Stocktons each were expert with guns. Without even taking aim Martin could bring a pomegranate down from a tree ten yards distant and Callie could keep a tin can in the air for as long as the ammunition in her weapon held out.

Watching this, Annie had a vision of herself in her front yard back home, shooting up cans, bouncing them around in the air, oblivious to the gaping, admiring sidewalk audience. The men of the town, the Lions and Rotarians and Saturday-night card players, would marvel at her skill and dexterity. They would say, "Buddy, that's one little gal I just wouldn't care to fool with. She's another Annie Oakley, the Peerless Lady Wingshot, the best markswoman this side of the Rockies. The other side, too, for that matter. She could put this town on the map if her father would allow it but he protects her from publicity." And the women—Suedella's mother and Gwendolyn's mother—would jerk Suedella and Gwendolyn around and pinch them and hiss, "Now why can't you do that? Look at her; she's magnificent. Oh, stop that whining. I don't want to hear any of your lame-brained excuses. Go home and do the dishes."

She, Annie, would be better than Callie. She'd keep *two* cans in the air with her gun. She'd keep one about three feet above Suedella's head and one about four feet above Gwendolyn's head and when her smoking gun finally stopped the cans would fall down and hit both girls on the head and knock them out.

Her father did not like the Stocktons' shooting exhibitions. He drew Annie and Calvin to him and said, "I'm not criticizing Martin or Callie now but I don't want you interested in this. Guns aren't playthings and there's nothing glamorous about them. They're lethal weapons."

"Lethal?" whispered Calvin and looked questioningly at Annie.

"Lethal means deadly," said Doc Jelks. "Even in the hands of an expert guns sometimes fire at the wrong time and kill people. Guns are not for people like us. Don't ever let me catch either of you even touching one with your little finger. You understand?"

Annie's dream of herself as the modern Peerless Lady Wing-shot dissolved. Standing spraddle-legged in the yard, plugging away at the tin cans, Callie struck Annie as being a silly woman. She's ignorant, thought Annie.

My father as much as said so just now. She should be in the house studying her cookbooks or doing something else womanly. No, she doesn't have any cookbooks. She doesn't have *any* kind of books. I wonder what she thinks about when she's not talking. I wonder what she and Uncle Martin talk about when they're by themselves. Probably nothing. There's nothing for them to talk about because they haven't learned anything new since they were young. As old as he is Uncle Martin still thinks the sun goes around the earth. Even Calvin knows it's the other way around. When I get back home I'm going to read up on planets. I know Calvin's right, he always is. It's just awful to be as ignorant as I am. To have to have some little kid tell you that horses don't eat meaty bones and that the sun doesn't go around the earth. I wish I had something to read.

The desire for something to read was, that afternoon, just a little annoying fragment, a slow, gentle nibbling at the idle layers of her mind. It was a dumb nuisance.

It was a piece of serendipity really, to be free of the lately acquired habit of running to the dictionary every five minutes. Serendipity? Curses. Now just what cretin had implanted *that* word in her mind when she wasn't looking? That old library baboon Miss Dishman probably. That old purveyor of happy, innocent minds. No, not purveyor. Predator. Miss Dishman was a predator of children's happy, innocent minds, spurring them on to think there was power in her old dusty books—actually telling them that. Power, bah! The only power you got from books was bigger arm and leg muscles. It took a lot of *that* kind of power to stagger to the library every other day and then stagger home again loaded down with a ton of books.

Seated on a flower pot in the scuppernong arbor Annie rolled her shirt sleeves back and tried to make her biceps swell but they wouldn't. The muscles in her arms were smooth and flabby. She reached up and picked a handful of grapes and ate them, sliding the skins around in her mouth, savoring the juice, crunching the slightly bitter seeds. She let her mind and her eyes wander. At the far end of the arbor there was a slatted bench containing an assortment of gardening tools, empty cans, and pasteboard boxes. Annie rose and sauntered toward the bench. One of the cans which had contained pumpkin-pie filling still had its recipe label. "Ah," said Annie and with a little bump of sharp, unexplained pleasure lifted the can and lovingly held it. She read its stained label twice. She cared nothing for the recipe; it was the words she was after and this was an astonishing thing.

On the sixth day of this visit Annie woke to a pure, still silence. The sun, striking through the windows, told her that it was an hour or two past dawn. There weren't any sounds from the kitchen or from any other part of the house.

Annie sat up and then rolled herself from her bed and stood up. During the night either her paunch had shrunk or else the elastic in the waistband of her pajamas had stretched. She went to the dresser mirror and regarded her image. The paunch was still there but decidedly it was smaller; the elastic in the top of her pajama trousers was still crisp and new. She pumped her legs and flexed her upper arm muscles and spoke to herself, her only true friend: *Oh, Catherine Rosalind, you are soooooo ugly.*

A note on the kitchen table said that the Stocktons and her father had gone to town for supplies. It didn't say anything about Calvin. She looked in his room and saw that it was empty. She went to the front porch and looked out across the fields. On the rise of land beyond the haystack the brown cows were peacefully grazing; the sky was delicately blue. A gray, neckless owl, perched behind a wag of Spanish moss in the buckwheat tree, peered out and blinked.

In her shower Annie composed a poem:

THE OWL IS A BIRD
WITH GREAT GOGGLE EYES.
HE IS WISE,
TO MY SURPRISE.

Catherine Rosalind Kingston provided music suitable to the lyric and Annie, standing under the tepid stream of water, made herself a white, glistening soap cap and sang, "The owwwwwwl is a birrrrrrd with great goggle eyes. He is wiiiiiise, to my surrrrrrprise."

The water and shampoo soap was in her ears so that the sound of her voice, high and off-key was muffled. There was another sound coming from somewhere,

coming through the house from the back yard. It wasn't
a scream nor yet even a cry. It was a long, unwinding,
chilling wail.

Annie stood quite still and listened and the soap and
water poured down over her neck and face and the
wailing didn't stop.

She stuck her head through the slit in the shower curtains and yelled: "Calvin! Calvin! Is that you out there?
I'm taking a shower. What're you yelling about?"

There came Calvin's acute, terrorized reply floating
through the rooms and corridors of the house, filling
them: "Annie! Annieeeeee! It's the crazy bull! He's out
here and he's got me. . . . Oh, help, somebody! The
crazy bull! He's crazy! He wants to kill me! Annieeeeee!"

Without turning off the water Annie left the shower
stall. Her foot caught on the loose rubber mat on its
floor and she almost fell. She grabbed her shorts and
shirt from the hook on the back of the door and thrust
her wet body into them and there was soap in her eyes
and her ears and her mouth. She ran through the house
to the back of the door shrieking. "Curses! That bull's
crazy, Calvin! Callie said so! He'll kill you! I don't
know how to rescue anybody from a bull, you little pug-
ugly! What'd you do to . . . ohhhhhh! Oh, curses!"

She had reached the back screen door and the snort-
ing, heaving, pawing, mad bull was in the yard stalking
around the tree Calvin was in. To Annie the bull looked
insane. His bitter mouth dripped white strings of saliva,
his short horns and his head were bloodied and there was

blood in his mean eyes. The tree in which Calvin was standing had blood on its battered trunk. Above this, among the green foliage, Calvin stood precariously frozen and the owl from the buckwheat tree out in front of the place had come to be a solemn, impassive witness. He was above Calvin's head on a higher branch sleepily looking down.

Annie saw the bull and Calvin and the owl all with one look. A ground swell of fear and inadequacy bit sharply into her. She pushed the screen door open an inch or so and the bull swung his head around; his eyes connected with hers. "No," she whispered. "No. You can't do this. Go away. Let us alone."

In the tree Calvin whimpered and the bull dragged his glance away from Annie, raised his eyes, and focused them on Calvin. He backed away from the tree and then charged. The tree swayed and Calvin's face, already drained white, turned whiter. His arms were around the tree tightly and his glasses were hanging from one ear. He had stopped wailing and whimpering.

In a cloud of helplessness and indecision Annie watched the bull back away to the farthest corner of the yard. She tried to measure the tree's capacity to withstand another assault. It looked old and brittle. The bull's full weight against it could surely bring it down. She thought of her slingshot in the trunk of her father's car and boiling water. No, to boil water to throw in the bull's face would take too long. He wasn't going to wait for anything, not anything. Already he was tired of fooling around. Heaving and panting and pawing at the earth, gathering his mad, massive strength, he was getting ready to charge the tree again. And Calvin was so silent up there in it, so awfully silent.

Annie whirled and ran the length of the house to the Stocktons' bedroom. Their guns were lying on a chest beneath the open windows. Without making a selection she picked up the nearest one, feeling but not being aware of its unexpected weight. Her rough, bare feet were weightless, too.

Now she stood in the screen door at the rear of the house, holding the door open with one foot and rigidly holding the gun out from her with both hands and screamed at the bull. "Bull! Bull! You wanna fight? Come on, pick on somebody your own size! Come on, come on! You're the one started it! Hyaaaaaah! That's right! Look at me! Forget the tree! I'm more interesting! Hyaaaaaah! You know what I'm going to do to you? I'm going to blow your brains out! Come on, come on! Hyaaaaaah! Hyaaaaaah!"

Through and through mad at the bull, at the situation, at the circumstances which had placed her in this situation, at Norma going her own immaculate way out in Hollywood, California, at all the mules and baboons in her life—the old people rocking and gossiping on the porch of The Gray Moss Inn back home, the Jacksons and the Rosses and the men of her town who excluded the Jelkses from church and her father from Saturday-night card games—Annie viciously pushed the screen door wide and jumped out on the porch. "Bull, I'm going to put a bullet in your crazy brain! Come on, come

on! Let's get it over with! You're the one started it, not
me! You're the one likes to pick on little kids! I didn't
tell you to! Hyaaaaaah! Hyaaaaaah!"

The bull was coming at her, was thundering toward
her. His head was down and he was coming straight at
her and Calvin was screaming, "Annieeeeee! Annieeeeee!" With both hands she raised the gun, training
it at the bull's head, and fired. The bull staggered to his
knees and rose. She fired again and again and again and
finally, within three feet of her, the bull lay dead. She
walked up to him and hurled the gun down on him.
"Lousy bull! *That'll* teach you to pick on little kids. I
guess you won't do it again, huh?"

Calvin was out of the tree and running toward her.
His glasses were crazily swinging from one ear and his
shorts were ripped and he was gasping tears. "Oh,
Annie, the bull would've killed me. I didn't do anything
to him . . . I was just out here looking around at things
and he came. . . . I didn't hear him coming . . . and
then I went up the tree. . . . Oh, Annie."

She pushed his hot, sweaty hands away. "Oh, be quiet,
Calvin. You get on my nerves. Did I ever tell you that?
Well, you do. You get on my nerves. My father's going
to kill me when he gets back and it'll be your fault. He
told me never to touch a gun not even with my little
finger and here I've gone and disobeyed him."

"Maybe," whispered Calvin, "we should bury the
bull. I could dig the hole. Then nobody would have to
know about him."

Annie said, "Yeh, Calvin, that's a good idea. You dig

the hole and we'll bury the bull. He only weighs about three tons. We can manage it. We'll get some ropes and drag him to the hole when you get it dug and then we'll cover him all up nice and nobody'll know that I killed him. No, wait a minute. I've got a better idea. Let's cut him up first. That way he won't be so hard to handle."

"Cut him up," whispered Calvin doubtfully. "Yes, we could do that. Maybe. Look at his head; it's awfully big. What will we do? Saw it off?"

"Oh, shut up, Calvin," said Annie. "Just shut up. I'm trying to think of what to tell my father when he comes home. I guess I'll just have to tell him the truth. He'll kill me but I guess I'll just have to tell him the truth."

"The truth," whispered Calvin. "Yes, you'd better tell him the truth. It always saves a lot of trouble."

Annie limped to the back steps and went up them. She banged the screen door behind her and went back to her shower. She stood under the warm water and let it flow over her. She started to shake and had to lean against the walls of the shower stall. I am not a nice girl, she thought. Nice girls don't kill bulls.

She wept.

CHAPTER TEN

THIS SUMMER WAS almost completed though in the full heat of the days the temperature still climbed to the high nineties. The bay tree in the Jelkses' front yard put out a final burst of bloom and the newspaper reported a hurricane in the Caribbean. Every afternoon it rained and afterward the streets and yards of the neighborhood would steam. These rains kept Annie from her hammock which had become a favorite loafing place. Because they were usually accompanied by dangerous lightning she was obliged to wait them out inside the house and be pestered by Calvin and Ruth.

Her ambition to become a famous writer had dwindled to a vague, helpless shred. She sat in her father's office-bedroom and stared at the typewriter and was uninspired. Soon school would start and every day she would have to escort Calvin to and from it and bear the looks and whispers. Her dream of becoming a judo or karate expert had faded, too. She could no longer picture herself fighting in the street with Suedella Jackson or Gwendolyn Ross. For some queer reason the desire to maim Suedella, to spit on her and tear her hair out by the roots and half kill her, had flown.

It was the bull's fault; killing him had done this to her. An account of this had been published in the local paper. She had posed for a photographer and had talked earnestly with a reporter for a full hour—giving him all the facts of her heroism:

"Were you scared?" he asked.

"Sure. But I don't want you to publish that I was. You can just say I was a little nervous. And that wasn't the bull's fault. It was Calvin's. He was up in that tree screaming his head off and that owl was up there, too; I don't know why. I always thought owls slept in the daytime. But anyway there I was and that old bull had it in his mind to murder me. He was big as this house almost. Well, with the first bullet I knocked his front teeth out—"

"His front teeth," said the reporter and his hand which had been writing, paused.

"Yes. The first bullet knocked them out. They fell to the ground. I never saw such big teeth. He snarled at me and kept coming. I pulled the trigger again. BANG! He jumped straight up into the air and jerked around backwards. I put another bullet into him. BANG! This one opened him up and some of his guts . . . wait a minute. Don't say I mentioned guts. It isn't a nice word. What's another word for guts?"

"Intestines," suggested the reporter.

"Yes. Intestines. So anyway this bullet . . . how many bullets have I told you about?"

"Three," murmured the reporter and took a handkerchief from his pocket and mopped his face.

"Okay. Maybe we'd better start over. The first bullet knocked out his teeth, see? And the second one spun him around and his intestines . . . listen, I don't think we'd better write about his intestines falling out. It's too gory. Skip what the second bullet did to him. Just say it jerked him backward. Then I fired the third bullet. BANG! He twitched sideways and his rump . . . no, not rump. We'd better not say rump. What's another word for rump?"

"Ah, rear," supplied the reporter.

"Yes. Rear. Oh, he had a big rear! You know what I thought about when I saw it? Xerxes."

"Xerxes?"

"Xerxes. I am talking about Xerxes the First. You'd better write that down so people will know. Because there were a lot of other guys named Xerxes. I mean Xerxes number one, the son of Darius number one and Atossa, the daughter of Cyrus the Great. I read a lot when I'm not working on the book I'm writing. I just love Xerxes and the bull's rump . . . his rear made me think of him. I go to the library every other day and bring home as many books as I can carry. I read every word in every one and then I take them back and get some more. I'll bet you I've read about two hundred books this summer. William the Conqueror is another guy I think I'm going to like. Miss Dishman recommended him to me."

The reporter was pushing his hands through his wiry curls. "About the bull. We'd better finish talking about him."

"Oh, yes. Well, I pumped about thirteen bullets into him and he died and that's all. I don't think guns are glamorous; they aren't playthings. My first name is Annie just like Annie Oakley, The Peerless Lady Wing-shot but I wouldn't want to be like her. I don't think she was so much, running around shooting off guns. I'll bet she never read a book."

"Thirteen bullets," the reporter was saying. "What kind of a gun was this you used?"

"I don't know. I think Callie said it was a .38 police special. She uses it on tins cans which I think is kind of dumb but you don't need to quote me. She and her husband are my father's friends but I don't think we'll ever visit them again."

"A .38 police special only holds six bullets," said the reporter.

"Really? Well, maybe I only pumped six bullets into the bull. But anyway I killed him. You can say I'm mod-est about it if you want. It wasn't I who phoned your paper about this. It was my nephew. I don't desire any publicity about it."

The photographer who had taken her pictures and was now sitting in the car at the Jelkses' curb was beck-oning. The reporter said thanks and good-bye and left and Annie went inside to her father's office-bedroom. The session with the reporter had queerly exhausted her. It had been her suggestion that Calvin phone the newspaper to tell them about the bull. She had thought the interview would be exhilarating but it hadn't gone exactly according to plan. It had run away from her. Telling the reporter all that stuff about Xerxes and the bull's big rear . . . that hadn't been a bit clever. Annie sat at the typewriter and tried to think of a story to write but no ideas came. She slitted her eyes and fingered her hair and felt her feet growing. It started to rain and the room grew dim and she left it.

She stood at the living-room windows and watched the rain splashing in the street. Suedella Jackson and Gwendolyn Ross, both in cute rain hats and raincoats sauntered past. They didn't look in the direction of the Jelkses' house. From a somber, inner region of Annie's mind there came a truth: Even when they read about me in the paper it won't make any difference, she thought. I could throttle *ten* bulls to death with my bare hands and it wouldn't make a bit of difference. Because that's the way they are; they want it this way. They enjoy it. If all of us—me, my father, Calvin, and Ruth—all sickened and died from the way they've gossiped about us they wouldn't even come to the cemetery to kick our bones. They're so right about everything.

Lonely and vaguely depressed, Annie went to her room and switched on all the lights. She sat on the edge of her bed listening to the rain on the roof and staring at the stack of library books on her dresser. She hadn't read any of them; she hadn't read anything for days and days except cereal labels at breakfast time.

The books drew her. She went to them and selected the one about William the Conqueror, King of Eng-

land, born 1027 or 1028. He was the illegitimate son
of Robert the Devil, duke of Normandy. His mother
was Arletta, daughter of a tanner.

On another day in this time Annie had a conversation
with Miss Dishman concerning the book about William
the Conqueror. "He was illegitimate," Annie said. "And
yet he got to be King of England. Isn't that amazing?
Isn't that the most amazing thing you ever heard?"

"No," replied Miss Dishman, arranging a bouquet of
marigolds. "Some of the things I hear and see today
amaze me much more than William the Conqueror ever
did."

Annie leaned against Miss Dishman's counter and
watched Miss Dishman's hands fuss with the green stems
and the orange flowers. The afternoon rain was at the
windows and the unpeopled library contained queer,
friendly odors. No, not odors. Scents. The scents of
other ages, glorious and inglorious. And distant places.
The silent diaries of the human race.

Annie turned and looked at Calvin who was squat-
ting at one of the low book shelves. He held an open
book and was raptly reading. He was smiling and nodding and in a minute he eased his little haunches to the
floor. There was light on his head; it shone like tinsel.

Miss Dishman had finished with the marigolds. She
was putting them on the shelf beside her telephone. She
was saying, "Many famous and successful people in
history have been illegitimate. Of course that's no cri-

terion for success and fame; I don't mean to imply that it is."

Annie shifted her weight from one foot to the other. She sighed and her eyes went to the dictionary on the stand beneath the windows. The rain had diminished— it was stopping—and Calvin had risen to come to the desk. He had selected so many books to take home she had to help him carry them.

Calvin wanted to stop at the drugstore for a hot fudge sundae or a Cherry Smash but she said, "Oh, Calvin, don't you ever think of anything besides your stomach? We haven't got time for that now." She hurried him around the corner and down the street. They went past The Gray Moss Inn and the old people on its porch leaned forward in their rockers and clucked their tongues.

"Why do they do that?" Calvin asked.

"Because they're ignorant," Annie answered. "They never heard about William the Conqueror. I've been wondering something, Calvin. I've been wondering if you'd ever thought about changing your name. Have you?"

"No," said Calvin, splashing through a puddle. "I never have. I'm glad I wore this hat. Now it's so hot."

"I've been thinking about changing your name to William. Just in private, I mean. When you go to school of course your name would have to be Calvin but at home you could be William. Wouldn't you like that? Don't you think William sounds . . . regal?"

157

Under the hat Calvin's head wagged. "I don't know. I don't know what regal means."

"Regal means kingly. It means like a king."

"Well," said Calvin. "I guess that'd be all right. But aren't people who're named William called Bill?"

"Oh, for heaven's sake, Calvin. You don't get the idea at all, do you? Why can't you just ever agree to what I say? Why do you always have to ask so many questions about my ideas? William is a lovely name. It's regal. A king of England once had it. From now on, in private, your name is going to be William and that's final."

Calvin skipped through another puddle and his bush hat slipped down to cover his forehead. He asserted himself. "No, I will not let you change my name to William, Annie. I will let you change it to Bill but not William. If you call me William I will not answer you but if you call me Bill, I will. And that's final."

Bill the Conqueror and Catherine Rosalind Kingston left the sidewalk and entered the vacant lots. They went home and sat for a while under the warm dampness of the oak trees. Drops from the overhead foliage dripped down on their heads and ran down the backs of their necks. They sat and talked a little about mild things, until Bill the Conqueror remembered his thirst and Catherine Rosalind remembered the word criterion. They lugged all their books inside and Bill the Conqueror went to the kitchen to make a pitcher of red iced drink with lemon wheels floating around in it.

Ruth had the vacuum cleaner out and was haphazardly cleaning the living room. She was singing one of her loud, annoying songs and when Annie went past her she grinned and raised her voice to a higher pitch.

In Calvin's room Catherine Rosalind consulted the dictionary but couldn't confine herself to just the word *criterion*. There were so many others—*crissum* and *cristate* and *criticaster* and *crocin*. It was maddening.

Catherine Rosalind Kingston fingered her hair and patted her ears. She rocked back and forth on her tough, bare feet and felt them growing. Itchy, nervous bumps appeared on her neck and cheeks. She rubbed them.

Annie Jelks, alias Catherine Rosalind Kingston, knelt before the thick dictionary. She flipped the pages faster and faster and read the words and their meanings savagely. "Curses," she said aloud. "All these words to learn and already I'm over twelve. Why didn't I start earlier? Oh, curses, I'll never get it all done."

Calvin was playing with his anatomy man, tiptoeing around it, putting all the organs in the right holes. And finally Ruth had remembered the song about the snake who grew tame and wanted to be caressed; she was singing it.